Nickel Miseries

Nickel
Miseries

A Collection

IVAN
GOLD

New York

THE
VIKING
PRESS

Published in *1963* by The Viking Press, Inc.
625 Madison Avenue, New York *22*, N.Y.

Published simultaneously in Canada by
The Macmillan Company of Canada Limited

Library of Congress catalog card number: *63-11860*

Some of the stories in this volume appeared originally, in somewhat different form, in the following publications: *New World Writing 4* ("A Change of Air"); *Esquire* ("The Nickel Misery of George Washington Carver Brown"); and *The Noble Savage 4* ("Kimiko's Tale").

M B G · *Set in Janson type and*
Printed in the U.S.A. by Vail-Ballou Press Inc.

For Artie and Syd

Contents

Nickel Miseries

A Change of Air

PROLOGUE

*B**obbie Bedmer* at the age of nineteen during the course of three warm August days and nights lost not her virginity which she had long before misplaced in the back of an automobile but the memory of it, and almost, along with this, the capacity to remember. What she knew when she awoke on the first of the August mornings was that on such a fine sunny morning one had to be completely out of one's head to go to work in a button factory what with a hundred better nicer cleaner things to do, and damn her mother and the button factory, she would go for a long walk out of doors or maybe to a movie. What she knew as well (but not as loudly) as her not going to work was exactly where she was going and why. But what she did not know . . . what she could not possibly know when

1

she got on the bus (which passed one park and two movie houses on its journey along an avenue of New York's lower East Side, but which also stopped almost directly outside the clubroom of the silk-jacketed Werewolves, membership thirty-five, and many friends) was that when she returned home seventy-two hours later, she would do so minus her underwear, the greater part of her emotional stability, her future in the button factory, and eleven pounds.

For the two or three young men of her acquaintance whom she expected to find in the clubroom at this early hour (they living there, being otherwise unhoused and temporarily unemployed) she found in the clubroom, running win, place, and show in a fabulous, all-night, seven-man stud-poker game, and consequently filled to overflowing with philanthropy (love for one's fellow man). She walked in boldly, then hesitated, seeing seven card players and three hecklers, ten in all, counted on Tony, Frank, and Fat Andy for the protection she thought she wanted, found them extremely interested in her presence, but averse to any plan of action which did not include their intimates at the card table, who were now poorer (and they richer) by three hundred dollars. Decided finally, persuaded by Frank's embraces and the uniqueness (ten of them—why not the hecklers too—on the same day) of the prospect, communicated her decision by her slightly hysterical laugh, running crazily up the scale and halfway down, and thereby set out to make East Side of New York (and possibly national) history.

For . . . although unrecorded in the Werewolves' minutes, or in any other written source (ignoring the possibility that one or more of the half-dozen or so twelve- to fifteen-year-old young men she devirginized during the three-day period was sentimental enough to keep a diary), it is proved

beyond any doubt by an unchallengeable number of oral
affirmations that Bobbie Bedmer (although expressing some
desire to leave about four o'clock of the same afternoon
when the situation seemed to be getting out of hand) nevertheless was taken, or rather had, one hundred and sixty times
during seventy hours by a total of fifty-three persons (the
entire membership of the Werewolves, their younger
brothers and friends) of all nationalities and sizes, slept a
grand total of seven hours during the three days and nights,
consumed a bottle of milk, two of beer, a number of pretzels
and a ham sandwich, called her mother on the evening of
the first day to assure her that everything was under control and (it was Friday) she was spending the night at a
friend's house and did not know exactly when she would be
home, and returned home two and one-half days later when
one of the Werewolves, preparing to make the trip for the
fourth time, suddenly and concernedly noticed how peaked
she was. They put her on a bus at eight o'clock on Monday
morning, thoughtfully providing her with carfare, warning
her to keep it quiet which they did not have to do since
she truly bore them no animosity, and she returned home,
eleven pounds less of her, to her mother and to the police
who had preceded her by only twenty minutes, and fainted
in the doorway.

When she awoke, tight-lipped, in a hospital, heard the
doctor proclaim to the police and nurse the girl has suffered
an ordeal, been without food and raped many times, laughed
her crazy laugh, and had to say you screwy sawbones you
it wasn't rape and how many times and laughed the crazy
laugh for many minutes at the doctor's guess of thirty the
nurse's forty the police's fifty, told them how many times
(having kept a careful count), told them laughing crazily it
was all her own idea and she might have a go at it again,

but worth less than nothing to the forces of law and order
in the names and places department.

They sent her away. They had to. Her mother wrung
her hands, cursed her God and the memory of her husband.
They sent her away for two years. When she returned from
Rehabilitation School she had regained the eleven pounds and
five additional. There were other, apparently deeper changes.

Franklin Cripple DeTorres, carrying himself well at five
foot seven, absolutely sound of limb and body, derived his
middle name, twenty-five cents, and a good part of his reputation as a result of an encounter in (and with) a subway.
Always sure of himself, acutely conscious of his heritage—
Puerto Rico (for his birth and the year afterward), New
York, and bravery—never more so than at five a.m. on a
liquored Sunday morning, Cripple (Crip to his friends) con-
jectured aloud on the fate of his foot provided he left it
where it was, hanging over the parapet above the tracks, a
void soon to be filled by an incoming subway train.

His friends, not realizing the full extent of his courage,
liking him and wishing (in good spirits) to create the opportunity to apply to him a large number of defamatory
epithets (which they would be in a position to do when he
snatched his foot from danger), offered (one of them did)
the sum of twenty-five cents to the soon-to-be-martyred if
he left his foot there until and after the train arrived. It
was not the money which decided him, but the attitude
which prompted its offer. Placing his foot as far as the heel
(with which he clutched the edge of the parapet for sup-
port) out over the parapet, Cripple waited. The train came.
He did not even flinch, not until the train (with its agonized
conductor) hit him, and then he did not flinch but fell down
parallel to the tracks, landing on his elbows, the foot which

earned him the name the money the reputation seemingly unhurt, and shouted very loudly, unhysterically, but with great conviction, get me to the hospital.

His ten weeks in the hospital he found dull but not unbearable, being able to leaf through the books previously stolen from the bookstore where he stock-clerked, being always interested in culture, and favored daily by visits from his friends, the entire membership of the Werewolves, most calling his act of bravery the stupidest thing anyone had ever done, but all admiring, and the six weeks after that when he walked with an ever-lessening limp were just that, six weeks, so he suffered nothing finally except the money he did not make (more than compensated for by the quarter which he had framed and hung in the Werewolves' clubroom, threatening death and other penalties to anyone who removed it), and he gained a name which it seemed to outsiders should offend him, until they learned the manner of its origination.

On the day Bobbie Bedmer did not go to work, Frank Cripple DeTorres won one hundred and forty dollars. It was the largest longest most expensive poker game ever played in the Werewolf clubroom, it was the most money he had ever won, and although by no means feeling guilty (perhaps even seeing a way to call a halt to the contest before his luck began to change), Cripple, when he saw her walk in, felt that the least he could do for the boys he had taken over was to get them to the slut as long as she happened to be around. He was the first on line, then, as the affair began to mushroom (something he did not foresee but which did not make any difference), thirty-first, and again one hundred and sixth. He was sorry to hear that the girl had been sent to a reformatory.

When the Werewolves disbanded (after a police raid

which led to the twelve Werewolves present at the club spending some time at headquarters, and the two of them identified by the badly battered grocery proprietor remaining after the others were allowed to leave) Cripple devoted himself to intellectual pursuits, spending most of his evenings at Gelber's Chess Club on Seventeenth Street. He went usually with Joe Muñeco, or met him there. They were the only two young men (except for occasional visits from Joe's friends) in what was otherwise a storm center for the old. Together, these two, they either beat (they played well) or talked down every old man in the place.

A problem to Early Environmentalists (the key to personality lies in the first three or five or nine or eleven years), *Joseph Muñeco* (of whom they had never heard) spent the first three years of his life running around the streets of San Juan, Puerto Rico, the next fourteen years escaping policemen (for playing stickball on New York City streets and mugging usually close-to-penniless passers-by); then, having been expelled from three high schools (for non-attendance of classes and smoking marijuana), finally happening across a novel by Thomas Wolfe, impressed enough to read this author's entire works, discovering James Joyce, and in his twentieth year, and his fourth high school, becoming the editor (and first-prize winner in a national short-story contest) of his high-school literary magazine.

Made many friends in this high school (at home on all intellectual strata), fell in love with and was loved by the editor of the high-school newspaper (a Jewish girl of orthodox parents who were destined to object to their daughter's keeping company with a Gentile, and with a Spanish Gentile, and with one who looked so typically and unhealthily

Spanish), went to a city college (his girl and he), saw the girl every day and on Saturday nights, and devoted the rest of his social time alternately to Cripple (alone or with mutual acquaintances, members of the long-defunct Werewolves) and to his other high-school friends (the last high school), cream of the intellectual crop, the boys who read the books, who thought about writing them (as he did—although he only thought), and who by fairly frequent remarks pertaining to his dual heritage (the literate hoodlum, and variants, with lots of laughter, although he had for a long time now adhered to the straight and narrow path) contributed to the growth of his impassioned unusual campaign of self-justification.

Impassioned unusual campaign of self-justification . . . not with his girl Anne, with whom he was in love; nor with Cripple and with these friends with whom he fitted in so perfectly that there was no need of it; but with the others . . .

With *Phillip Zand*, literary critic until his junior year at college, thinking now of psychology, seeing it as a back door to the world he didn't live in; a great reader and a great listener to music, and a self-styled neurotic, finding himself replete with wrong things to say (to women), and not enough women to say them to; not pretty, but (not that this mattered) not as unpretty as he thought he was, weakly contemptuous of the others, his close circle of friends, in the only regions where he was qualified to be contemptuous, books and music, finding them in these regions, although reasonably well informed, nevertheless with sufficient (for the purposes of ridicule) misinformation . . .

With *Jay Miller,* a college man, sporadically read in
Schopenhauer, Nietzsche, and Philip Wylie, with some
Havelock Ellis (being interested in sex); contentious but
without a conciliatory delivery (far from it; always unpleasant, not going out of his way to be unpleasant, but
being that way because it came easiest), with the result
that among his group of friends he had no friend; cherubic
in appearance (and thus with a number of conquests to his
credit which Phil Zand—by no means accidentally—was
forever hearing about, but still . . .), a lecher at nineteen,
being famed (and given no peace) for the most amazing
collection of pornographic snapshots and literature perhaps
ever assembled, delighting in lending certain parts of his
collection to Phil since he knew what he used them for, a
good but strange mind; a flair for chess, a match for Joe
Muñeco, a terrific and serious rivalry building between
them, a result of and a further prod to mutual dislike . . .

With *Benjamin Brock,* the only one of them attending a
college which it required money to attend, assuming therefore a certain superiority in the quality of his education,
never having to mention the felt superiority for them to
know that it was there; doubting especially (again tacitly,
or if not tacitly, then blatantly in jest) Muñeco's claim to
higher understanding (Joe having not written since the days
of his high-school triumphs—Ben writing all the time—two
long years ago, unable to take his typewriter out of pawn,
and besides, being busy—with his girl and with Cripple—
being happy), Muñeco feeling Ben's doubts, and the doubts
of the others, knowing the realm of the intellect to be his
as well as (if not more than) theirs, but feeling it always
necessary to prove it to them, and so . . .

Joseph Muñeco's impassioned unusual campaign of self-justification, the utilization of a phenomenal memory, an almost photographic memory, committing to it the equivalent of three large volumes of verse, from Sappho to Cummings, and considerable prose, quoting some part of his repertoire at the least provocation, creating his own provocation, irrelevant (the quoting) to anything occurring or even said in his immediate environment, but illustrating to Phil and to Jay and to Ben and to anyone else around that he, Joseph Muñeco, had a sizable portion of the world's literature at his fingertips, had the best that man's mind has yet created stored (with an understanding of it, if anyone pursued the matter) in his memory, that he, Joseph Muñeco was, whatever else he might also be, an intellectual.

With this and these in mind, we can begin the story.

THE STORY

I

Gelber's Chess Club was partly that. More, it was a place to play cards and a place to stay, on cold winter nights and dull summer ones. In the back of the club, away from the two windows overlooking Seventeenth Street, was a small room with a stove in which Mrs. Gelber made and sold coffee and sandwiches. The long, large room which was the club was divided by common consent into the sections for chess players and for card players; there were the few benches in the chess-player section for those who wished to sleep, to think, or to read the paper. On the door of the club was a sign reading FOR MEMBERS ONLY and inside the club a sign said MEMBERSHIP DUES, ONE DOLLAR A YEAR. Neither of these mattered. Gelber was friendly, did not need the money, and owned the building. The signs were put up at the insistence of his wife and Gelber neither desired to, nor did he, reinforce them. The club had been on Seventeenth Street for twenty-two years, and although the faces changed, at intervals, the mean age of the members did not. The men at the club—and they were all men aside from Gelber's wife—averaged fifty-five years of age. If not for the presence of Joseph Muñeco and Franklin De-Torres, who came often enough to necessitate their inclusion in any mathematical calculations, the average age of the members of Gelber's Chess Club would have been fifty-seven.

Frank DeTorres was talking to Joe Muñeco.

"Okay Ace," he said. "Push the pawn. Before the place closes, Ace. I guarantee the safety of the pawn move."

Frank had arrived at eleven o'clock and had played chess with the old men. He won more than he lost and he enjoyed his conversation and the reactions to it. At one o'clock Joe Muñeco walked in, earlier than usual for a Saturday night, but his girl had gotten sick and he took her home early, leaving her a block from where she lived in case one of her parents happened to be looking from the window. Meeting her on Saturday nights was no problem since she had a job

ushering at concerts in a school auditorium in his neighborhood, and he could meet her afterward, at nine-thirty. On
this Saturday night she became ill and he took her home.
When he got to the club, he and Frank DeTorres played
chess. Muñeco was the better of the two but against each
other they played carelessly, and games were not won or
lost in accord with their ability.

At DeTorres' remark, Joe became angry for the three old
men who made up his audience.

"Take it easy, Ace," he said. "Any time you want to play
three seconds a move, you let me know Ace. The pawn
move is for the fushas. I give you this." He moved his
bishop along its diagonal. One of the old men grunted approval and smiled a toothless smile. Frank addressed him.

"Doesn't he play like a master?" he said. "He is a true
Morphy in the way he plays this game. I admire your
manipulation of the pieces, Ace," he said to Joe. He looked
swiftly at the board and made his move. "Try this on," he
said.

Joe guffawed. "Swish, Ace," he said, swooping down
upon DeTorres' unprotected queen, removing it, and up-
setting four or five pieces on both sides of the board.

"I didn't see, Ace," Frank said, beginning to smile. Two
of the old men laughed. The third yawned noisily and
moved toward one of the benches leaning against the wall.

Frank resigned. He began to set up his pieces in prepara-
tion for another game. At one-thirty Phil Zand and Jay
Miller walked in. They had gone to a movie, had coffee, and
come to the chess club looking for Joe Muñeco. They knew
that he could be found here on Sunday mornings at this
time after taking his girl home.

"Watch him!" Joe said agitatedly to Phil, glancing momentarily at Jay, as the two came over and sat down. "You shouldn't have taken him off the leash. He's liable to rape small boys."

"No need," Jay said. "I was refreshed last night. A very sweet young thing I met at a dance. How's Anne?"

The query might have been solicitous, but it was very poorly placed. Suddenly Muñeco was no longer amusing or amused.

"She's all right," he said, looking at Jay. "Unless you just killed her by mentioning her name."

Jay laughed. He laughed unpleasantly, the only way he knew how.

"I thought you had signed a non-aggression pact," Phil said.

"Only verbal," Joe said. "It can be busted at any time."

"What's new?" Frank said to Phil.

"I'm glad you asked," Phil said. "My profession. I'm going to be a psychologist."

"That's nice," Frank said. "We are in need of psychologists. But you've got to gain weight if you want to be healthy enough to pursue your studies. You're very thin, in spite of your weight-lifting."

Phil laughed.

" 'I am thy father's spirit,' " Joe said. " 'Doomed for a certain term to walk the night, and for the day confined to fast in fires, till the foul crimes done in my days of nature are burnt and purged away. But that I am forbid,' " he said, " 'to tell the secrets of my prison-house, I could a tale unfold whose lightest word would harrow up thy soul,' checkmate Ace," he said.

"You're a genius, Muñeco," Jay said, sitting in the chair Frank had just vacated. Frank visited Mrs. Gelber for some coffee.

"You didn't like that?" Joe inquired. "Maybe you'd prefer an excerpt from Krafft-Ebing. 'George K., longshoreman, locked in the embraces of Mollie F., housewife suffering from vaginismus, found it difficult to extricate . . .'"

"No moves back," Jay said, making his first move.

"Make it touch move," Joe said, unsmiling. "Better than that, we measure the Galvanic Skin Response. If I catch you thinking about a piece, you got to move it."

"Agreed," Jay said.

Phil laughed: at their seriousness, and at the incongruity which it seemed to him the technical term had in Muñeco's mouth.

"What do *you* know about the Galvanic Skin Response?" he said.

"Nothing," Joe said. "Now that you're a psychologist I know nothing about the Galvanic Skin Response. Just as when previously you were a literary critic I knew nothing about literature. And as in consequence of your large record collection, I know nothing about music. If I ever again say anything implying I know anything at all about psychology, may I suffer excruciating pain."

"Okay," Phil laughed. "I'm sorry. You're an intellectual."

Frank returned with his coffee. He knew these two, Jay and Phil, and also Ben, because of their friendship with Joe Muñeco. They had graduated from high school with Joe three years ago, and he had continued seeing them, about once a week, since then. They were not particularly interesting, Frank thought, although they were supposed to be bright, and he guessed that this was what Joe saw in them. He could talk to them in Joe's presence, but doubted if he could find anything to say to them under other circumstances. These never arose since he ran into them only when he was with Muñeco. Now he returned with the coffee and he saw skinny Phil leaning on the table, his hair mussed, smiling at Muñeco, and it stuck him what a particularly dull life Phil must lead.

"Hey Phil, you still got it?" he said.

"Got what?"

"Your chastity. Last time I heard, you had still got it."

"Still got it," Phil said, smiling ruefully, but resignedly, as if talking about an amputated arm.

"I can't understand it, Ace," Frank said. "What's the good of going to college if they don't teach you about life? That's why I didn't go to college, because they had no courses in screwing."

"That's right, Ace," Joe mumbled, engrossed in the game.

"You should have gone," Jay said. "You're a great loss to the academic world."

Frank had begun to understand that the things Jay said in jest were no different in tone from the things he said when he was being nasty. It was just the way he talked, everything seeming an insult. He thought for a moment, and decided from the context that Jay was jesting.

"I appreciate this," Frank said.

Frank sat down to kibitz the game, and Phil read the Sunday *Times*. If no one else arrived and even if someone else did, they would spend an hour or two at the chess club, then go downstairs and across the street into the all-night cafeteria (it was too cold in January for the groups to gather in Union Square Park), spend some time there over their coffee, and then go home at four or five o'clock in the morning. They would take Phil, who became tired before anyone else, and who lived the greatest distance (fourteen blocks) from Seventeenth Street, home first, then would walk three blocks uptown to where Jay lived; and

finally walk back to the chess club, and three blocks beyond
it, to the street on which Frank and Joe lived, in adjoining
tenement buildings.

But Ben Brock arrived. Even this wouldn't have made any
difference, for Ben Brock often arrived without noticeably
disturbing the Saturday-night ritual. But Ben Brock arrived
with the family car, which meant, if nothing else, that they
would all be driven home. It meant however enough more
than that on this Saturday night to change the entire texture
of the evening.

"Okay," he said, when he saw them around the chess
table. "Drop everything. The bus awaits. Let me take you
away from all this."

"You park it in the hallway?" Joe said.

"Stop, I can't stand the irony," Ben said. "The car is
parked downstairs, three picas from the curb. How many
times do I have to tell you, Muñeco, I can park a car?"

"Perhaps," Joe said. "As soon as Krafft-Ebing here resigns
his lost game."

"Lost game!" Jay said, angrily incredulous. "You talk
like a chess player," he said. "But rather than destroy your
ego, I agree to a ride in Brock's convertible."

"Anything," Phil said, "for a change of scenery."

Frank sat behind a board, set up the pieces, and beckoned
to an old man who sat, half dozing, on a bench. The old man
smiled and came toward him.

"Spot me a rook, Kurtz," Frank said.

The old man smiled. "Why not both?" he said. He sat
down opposite Frank.

"Hey Crip, you coming?" Joe said to him.

"You college men go for a ride in the car," Frank said.
"Driving . . ." (he groped for the cliché) ". . . exerts no

appeal on me. I'm gonna teach Kurtz here how to play this game." The others were already outside and down the one landing to the street.

"Okay Ace," Joe said. "Castle early and open up a rook file. I'll see you." He turned and walked toward the door.

"So long Ace," Frank said.

2

The car was riding north, along First Avenue, toward Forty-second Street.

"Are we going to Times Square?" Phil said.

"If that's what you want," Ben said. "Although I was going to drive you down to Miami. It's time you phony authors and literary critics and psychologists and perverts learned that the East Side of New York is not the center of the world."

"How do you know that?" Joe said.

"Hearsay," Ben said. "But it sounds logical."

"We'll go to Miami next time," Phil yawned. "I've got to wake up early tomorrow."

On the corner of Twenty-sixth Street Ben stopped for a light. Muñeco, sitting up front, glanced from the window. "Hey," he said suddenly. Ben, following Joe's eye, saw a figure turn the corner of Twenty-sixth Street and walk out of his range of vision. "Was that Barbara Bedmer?" Joe said.

"I don't know," Ben said. "Shall we find out?"

"Who's Barbara Bedmer?" Phil said.

"What difference does it make?" Jay said. "It's a girl's name."

The light changed and Ben turned the corner. "I've told you about her," Joe said, peering from the window. The street was dark and he could not be sure. "That's the girl they sent up for the impairment of everybody's morals. The record holder. I didn't know they'd let her out."

"Is it her?" Ben said, slowing down a few yards behind the girl.

"I can't tell," Joe said.

The girl turned off and walked up to a stoop leading to the entrance of a building.

"Well you'd better find out if you're going to find out," Jay said.

Joe opened his window.

"Barbara," he called. "Is that Bobbie Bedmer?"

The girl turned, startled. It was late at night and she had not heard the car turn the corner. She saw the car but could not see who was inside. The car was a 1950 model, a red convertible. Ben and his father had washed and polished it that same day. It looked like a new car. Bobbie Bedmer came, looking very curious, down the stairs and up to the open window.

"Hello," Joe said cheerfully. "I thought it was you. Do you remember me?"

"Yeah," Bobbie said, smiling blankly. "Yeah, I remember you. What's your name?"

Joe grinned. "Joe," he said. "I used to belong to the Were-wolves. Remember the Werewolves?"

Bobbie grinned innocently back at him. "Yeah, I remember," she said. "How is everybody? How's Fat Andy?"

"He's fine," Joe said. "He got caught with a stolen car. He won't be around for a while."

"Gee, that's a shame," Bobbie said, meaning it. She laughed. "How's Tony?" she asked.

"I haven't seen him around," Joe said. "I think he's in the Army. But where have you been all this while?" he asked her, knowing she would lie, anxious to see how badly. "I haven't seen you for a long time."

Bobbie giggled. "Oh, I been away. I just got back to New York last week."

"You live in this house?" Jay said to her.

For the first time she took notice of the other occupants of the car.

"Yeah," she said, wary, but not unfriendly. Then to Joe: "Who are your friends?"

"Shall I introduce you?" Joe said.

She nodded, laughing.

"Bobbie Bedmer," Joe said. "This is Brock, the driver and part-owner of the car. This is Miller," and he gestured toward the back of the car, "consultant in pornography, and this is Zand, who is interested in people."

Bobbie laughed, taking her cue from his tone. "What are you doing out so late?" she said. "Just driving around?"

"Yeah," Jay said, anxious to make his presence felt. "How about you?"

"I went to a dance," Bobbie said. "At the Twenty-eighth Street Y."

"Did you have a nice time?" Lee said.

"Not so bad," Bobbie said, laughing.

There was a pause. Ben thought he might as well. She was standing there with her hand resting on the edge of the lowered window.

"Would you like to go for a ride?" he said.

Bobbie laughed uncertainly. "I don't know," she said. "My mother expected me home early, and it's late already."

"So," Joe said, "if it's late already it won't hurt if you

come in a little later. Come on," he said persuasively, "we'll go for a ride."

"Where are you going?" the girl asked.

"We don't know," Ben said drily. "That's what makes it so exciting. We might go almost anywhere. Maybe you can help find us a destination."

The girl stood there, her hand on the window. Joe opened the door suddenly and beckoned to her. "Come on," he said. "Any place you say. When you're ready to come back, we'll bring you back."

"It's a nice car," she said.

Joe laughed. He reached out his hand and pulled her one step closer to the car. Then he let go and moved closer to Brock, making room for her. Bobbie Bedmer laughed and got into the car.

Ben backed the car to the corner and they were back on First Avenue. He rode to Fourteenth Street and stopped for a light.

"You're looking well," Joe said. "You're looking much better than when I saw you last."

"Yeah," Bobbie said. "I gained a lot of weight."

She had changed. She had gotten into the car, but it wasn't as easy as it once would have been. Joe decided to let De-Torres find out how matters stood with the girl. Although he could have done so, his friends might interpret his efforts as illustrating a lack of sensibility. Or it might give them something to laugh about.

"Drive back to the club," Joe said. "We'll pick up Cripple."

"What club?" Bobbie asked alarmedly. "Who's Cripple?"

"Just a chess club," Joe said soothingly. "You remember Cripple. That's Frank, Frank DeTorres. You remember Frank, don't you?"

"What do you want to see him for?" Bobbie said.

"We don't want to see him," Joe said. "We just thought after all this time, he would be glad to see you. He won't hurt you."

Bobbie laughed. "I know he won't hurt me," she said. "I just thought we were going for a ride."

"We will," Ben said, knowing what was on Muñeco's mind. "Just as soon as we pick up Frank."

He turned left on Seventeenth Street, pulled up in front of Gelber's Chess Club, and parked the car.

3

Frank was happy to have Muñeco back and happier still when he saw who was with him. The presence of Bobbie Bedmer, he felt sure, would liven up the evening. He thought immediately of his pigeon coop and its steam-heating. When Ben Brock came upstairs, after parking the car, he found Frank and Joe seated near the window, Frank talking earnestly to Bobbie, and Jay and Phil standing some distance away leaning against a chess table. He walked over to these two.

"Set 'em up," he said to Jay. "You can have the white pieces."

"I'll have to beat you in five moves," Jay apologized. "Don Juan is operating, and I don't know how long we'll be here."

"If he's got to operate," Ben said, "you may be here a long time. If this girl is the girl she's cracked up to be she should be on her hands and knees begging for it."

Joe came over.

"How does it look?" Jay said.

"I don't know," Joe said. "Frank is trying to get her to go to his place but she doesn't like pigeon coops."

"Ask her about bar-bell clubs," Phil said. "I've got the key to the club. There won't be anyone up there this time of night."

"I'll keep you posted," Joe said. He walked back to Frank and the girl.

"Your move," Jay said.

Ben looked at him. "I can't understand your hanging around, Miller," he said to him, "in the hope of laying a broad who has already been on intimate terms with everyone in the neighborhood. Haven't you got any standards?"

"Very funny," Jay said. "In this respect I'm like you. When it comes to women, anywhere and any time."

"Are you looking forward to this prospect?" Ben said to Phil.

"Why not?" Phil said.

"Hell," Ben said, "you've had it so long you might as well save it for your wife. Listen to me," he said earnestly, "and don't throw yourself away on this harlot. Somewhere, there's a sweet, young, innocent girl who has been ordained by heaven to . . ."

"Balls to you," Phil said.

Muñeco returned.

" 'The outlook wasn't brilliant for the Mudville nine that day,' " Joe began, with every intention of completing the poem.

"Can it," Ben said. "What's the latest?"

"She met a psychiatrist in reform school," Joe said. "He told her the reason she did what she did was her father died when she was six years old and she missed male attention. She agrees with his diagnosis and she's turning over a new leaf."

"You mean all the psychiatrist did was tell her?" Phil asked professionally.

"I don't know," Joe said. "She's been away for two years. Maybe she underwent intensive therapy. Whatever happened, she's metamorphosized."

"So?" Jay said.

"We're going to take her downstairs, try to soften her up," Joe said. "Give me the keys to the car," he said to Ben.

"You going somewhere?" Jay said suspiciously.

"Hey," Muñeco laughed, taking the keys from Ben. "You think we'd run out on you, Miller? We can't leave you. This whole party is in Phil's honor. After Phil lays her we're going to nail her over his fireplace for a trophy." He jingled the keys at DeTorres and walked to the door. Frank got up, took the girl by the hand, and followed Muñeco. She went without protesting but she did not look happy.

"Does Cripple have a driver's license?" Jay said.

Ben nodded.

"If those guys pull anything," Jay said, "I'm going to make Muñeco pay for it."

"You wouldn't tell his mother, would you?" Ben said.

"No," Jay said. "I'll tell his girl. I'll call his girl and let her know how Muñeco spends his Saturday nights." He looked toward the window. Phil, following his glance, walked over and looked out.

"The car's still there," Phil said. "Save your money."

"Your move," Ben said.

Jay moved.

"How long we going to wait here?" he said.

"Give them five more minutes," Ben said.

Phil walked over and looked out the window.

"Hey Zand," Ben called to him.

"What?"

"You're basing your life on a lie," Ben said. "You want to become a clinical psychologist. You want to help the maladjusted. Now here is this girl who has been abnormal, at least quantitatively, but has since been returned to normalcy by a practicing psychiatrist. Instead of trying to keep her there you're party to a scheme whose aim is to tear down her defenses and re-sink her in the morass of abnormality."

He looked sternly at Phil, then disgustedly shook his head.

"Look," Phil said. "Better her than me. She's neurotic from too much of it and I'm neurotic from too little. It's her or me. And I've got my career at stake."

"He thinks it's the panacea," Jay sneered. "Once he gets laid, he's solved all his problems. What an idiot."

"Okay," Ben said. "I resign. Let's go downstairs."

They got up and put on their coats. "Hey, Kurtz," Ben called to the old man who had been sitting on a bench watching them. "A lineup. Anybody else, we're charging two-fifty. For you, a buck and a half. How about it?"

The old man coughed up some phlegm and spit it into a handkerchief. He was unimpressed. "If I couldn't do better," he said, standing and stretching himself, "I'd shoot myself."

The three left the club.

4

Ben looked in at the back window of the car. Joe and Frank were in the front seat with the girl between them. Frank had his arm around the girl and was bending over her. Ben motioned the others to wait. After a while the girl worked an arm free from behind her and pushed Frank's face away. Ben walked to the side of the car and knocked on the window. Muñeco opened the door.

"Come on in," he said. "We'll go for a ride."

Jay and Phil got into the back of the car. Ben squeezed into the driver's seat. There were four people in the front of the car. Joe moved over, making room for Ben, at the same time pushing Bobbie closer to Frank. Frank was talking into her ear.

"What's the matter baby? Don't you want to kiss me? Just a little kiss?"

"No-oo," the girl said, indicating that she had said it many times before. Frank leaned over her and kissed her. After a great many seconds had passed she pushed his face away.

"I don't know what's happened to the way you kiss," Frank said to her. "It's not like you used to. Who ever heard of a girl kissing with her mouth closed?"

"I don't want to kiss you," Bobbie said primly.

"Two years ago," Frank said, "I wouldn't kiss you. I would screw you. That's more fun, isn't it? What's happened to you in two years?"

"I told you," Bobbie said, laughing. Her laugh was heavy, like her voice, and unsteady, but it was not the way she used to laugh. "I don't do that any more."

"For nobody?"

Bobbie laughed. "I don't know," she said. "But not for you."

"I'm truly sorry to hear that," Frank said. "I guess I'll go home and go to bed. Drive me home, Brock," he said. He leaned over the girl.

Ben made a right turn on Third Avenue and drove to Twentieth Street. He stopped once for a light. On Twentieth a sanitation truck was double-parked and he slowed down to squeeze past it. During all this time, Frank, using all his art, was kissing the girl.

"You're home," Ben said.

"Yeah," Frank said. "We're home. Come on," he said to the girl. "We'll go upstairs to the pigeon coop and have a party."

"No," Bobbie said. "I don't like pigeon coops."

"Do you like parties?" Joe said.

"Not that kind," she said, laughing slyly.

"Look," Frank said. "Look what I got for you." He took her hand and pulled it to him, but she wrenched it free.

"I don't want it," she said, annoyed. "Leave me alone."

Ben became slightly annoyed by the proceedings. Not by the proceedings as much as by their lack of success.

"All right Frank, you drew a blank," he said. "We forgive you. If you can't convince this girl, she cannot be convinced. Go to bed." He looked at Bobbie. "I'll drive you home."

"Okay," Frank said. "But I don't know what's happened to this girl. She goes away for a short time and comes back with a whole new system of values. It's something for you college men to figure out."

He got out of the car.

"Don't give up the ship," he said. "A little patience. If this girl is Bobbie Bedmer you should lay her before daybreak. I'm going to get some sleep."

The girl laughed as Frank turned his back and walked away. "Don't believe him," she said confidentially. "I don't do any of those things. He's just talking." She directed this primarily at Brock in whom she had mistaken the annoyance with DeTorres' methods for sympathy. Joe smiled. Ben started the car.

"Who's going home first?" he said.

"Home?" The girl was indignant. "I thought we were going for a ride."

"You still want to go for a ride?" Ben said.

"Sure. Let's go to Coney Island."

"No," Joe said to her. "Let's go lift some weights. Phil has the key to his bar-bell club."

The girl laughed. "Ah, die young," she said pleasantly. She recognized that the only serious threat had been Frank, and he was gone. She relaxed now, and looked forward to a good time being chauffeured around.

"You can drive me home," Phil said, seeing the futility of remaining. "I've got to wake up early tomorrow."

"How about you, Miller?" Ben said.

"No hurry," Jay said. "As a matter of fact you can take me home after you drop her off."

The girl laughed. "You ain't gonna miss nothin'," she said.

Joe laughed. "You're a dead pigeon, Miller," he said. "Even this dumb broad reads you like a book. You're shallower than a wading pool."

"That's extremely funny, Muñeco," Jay said.

"I'm not a dumb broad," Bobbie said good-naturedly.

"Then what are you a dumb?" Joe said.

"Oh, die young," the girl said.

"Where would you like to go *besides* Coney Island?" Ben said.

"What's the matter with Coney Island?"

"There is nothing open and nobody in Coney Island in January," Ben explained patiently. "So I suggest you suggest something else."

"Let's go where there's excitement," Bobbie said. "Maybe we can see a fight somewhere."

"We have just the thing for you," Joe said. "Take her to Brooklyn," he said to Ben.

"That's right," Ben said. "Brooklyn's a wild town."

"What's so wild about Brooklyn?" the girl said.

"Everything goes positively smash in Brooklyn," Ben said. "There's a fight on every street corner. Trunk murders take place in front of your eyes. Also, there's a little cafeteria right across the bridge where we sometimes sober up after a devil-may-carish Saturday night."

"What's *his* name?" Bobbie said to Joe.

"That's Brock," Joe said. "Author and professional chauffeur. Why, do you like him?"

Bobbie laughed. "He's all right," she said.

"Brock has made a conquest," Jay called from the back of the car.

"I guess you're not interested," Joe said. "Maybe we should drive you home."

"Maybe you should," Jay said. "As a matter of fact, I'm sure you should. I've got a date tomorrow night with this girl I just met. I can use some sleep."

"You poor kid, I'll bet she knocks all hell out of you," Ben said.

Ben turned left, a block before the bridge which led to Brooklyn, and brought the car back to First Avenue. He left Phil on the corner of Third Street, and drove Jay to his home on Sixth Street between First and Second Avenues. He was tired, and got to thinking of the difficulty he would have in finding a parking space.

"Who's next?" he said.

He looked at Bobbie, who was about to protest.

"My old man gets up early in the morning," he lied. "He needs the car to get to work. I've got to bring it back before six o'clock."

"Gee," the girl said. "Your father works on Sundays?"

"Yeah," Ben said. "He's a preacher."

"Gee, that's tough," the girl said.

"Take me home first," Joe said, winking at Ben. "She said she likes you. Don't you like him, Bobbie?"

"Yeah, I like him," Bobbie said. "But I just wanted to drive around."

"You first," Ben said to her. He drove her home.

She got out of the car and turned toward them.

"Well, so long," she said. She laughed suddenly. "I had a very nice time."

"Glad to hear it," Joe said. "We must get together sometime and do the whole thing over again."

Ben leaned over and waved to her. "So long Bobbie," he said.

"By-by Brock," she said. "It was nice meeting you." She walked up the stoop and was gone, into the building.

They sat there for a while, not talking.

"A hundred per cent American girl," Ben said finally. "I'm convinced you had her pegged wrong."

"A hundred and sixty times," Joe said absently, "in three days. That must have been one hell of a psychiatrist."

"He wasn't an East Side boy," Ben said, shaking his head. "He performed a great disservice to an entire neighborhood. He dissolved the last trace of communal endeavor to which we could proudly point."

"Yeah," Joe said, leaning back on the seat, his hands locked behind his head. "Drive around to Seventeenth Street. What we've got to do now is get some coffee."

Kimiko's Tale

I SING of bits and parts of Helen, a nervous type with an admirable genealogy. I celebrate a few aspects of her psyche that read fairly well, naturally not all of those. Her constant companions were nightmares, aliases, and three pairs of breasts, these last acquired through the Ladies' Section at the U.S. Post Exchange. One mentions also her legs, not precisely broomstick thin, thus cutting the ground from under those remarking her resemblance to a witch, the peaked cheekbones in the long, narrow face, the slanted and scrutable eyes. I call attention to her freckles, her cleverness, her aspirations, her lungs. I sing of her ensnarement, poor butterfly, in the net of an unsubtle incarnation, a rowdy stop-over made in the fifties by her busy, migrant soul. In short I underline her palpability, rendering obscure the eternal aspects, giving no doubt more than its due to this frantic fleeting world.

I met Kimiko for the first time (check one:) in an airplane over the Grand Canyon, at a K.K.K. meeting, on the

banks of the Yangtze, in the court of Godaigo; I met her
in a democratic dream, and sometime thereafter she told
this story:

Listen, Blakesan, to an amusing if somewhat macabre
tale. On the Saturday night after payday of the Fourth
Moon, when Sixstripes had not turned up by six-fifteen, it
occurred to me that he might not come at all, which would
make it only the second Saturday since discovering the Snakepit that he had failed to stop by. I wondered what could
have detained him, and while I am no expert on the work-
ings of the U.S. Army, in my own country or another's, I
concluded that it must have been another girl, since it had
been my experience that very little apart from his own
interests and large-scale events (and there were none to
speak of at the time) could prevent an unmarried supply
sergeant (three up and three down) from keeping a date
on a payday Saturday night. My first reaction was of amusement, anticipating the difficulties I might raise in the face
of any subsequent attempt to account for his whereabouts
this evening, mostly, I admit, as a favor to him, because
he loves to apologize. I recall the evening I was delayed
by a medical and reached the Pit after eleven; he was already
engaged with Sally, who should have known better. That
brought on two remorseful weeks and some nylons from
the PX (for which he swore he had to borrow a friend's
wife's ration book—I see no reason to doubt him), but on
that occasion I was really angry, although less at him than
at the girl. She, too, apologized, claimed to have drunk so
much as to have forgotten protocol, or even the fact that
Sixstripes was and had been for eight months my regular
Sabbath customer; to this I replied, "Don't shit me!" and
complicated her life for some time to come. Seniority de-

mands respect. I've been at the Snakepit since before it had
a name, and all through the time when the one it had was
apposite.

I sing in this footnote of the Snakepit, home of fun and
fantasy, home of Helen-Lola-Kimiko-Toshiko and dozens
more, with less *Sitzfleisch* and fewer names. I celebrate its
function, location; I salute in passing its patrons, its prices,
its decor. But largely I deal with it here to forestall Helen:
she'd traduce it by romance, she'd mock it with praise.

Its name: where the fruit stand now stood had once been
a store that sold snakes. This trade in Japan is in a state of
decline, particularly in the large cities, where the snake has
been replaced, aphrodisiacally and medically, by respec-
tively shorter skirts and the family drug store, and the pro-
prietors of this particular shop moved elsewhere, but not
before a christening had taken place in the rear structure for
which the snake store (and now the fruit stand) was but
a façade: a bottle of Nippon beer brought down with great
force and no little sentiment across the leg of the organ in
the upstairs waiting room, and the Snakepit was born. The
sergeant responsible for the baptism had long since departed,
as had his entire era, but the name remained, along with the
faded calligraphy over the entrance, recalling the reptile
traffic of a bygone day. Kimiko had been present at this
ceremony. Unacquainted with its richness, she was none-
theless struck by the name, and was in some ways responsible through the years for its perpetuation.

Location: behind the above-cited fruit stand on the second
busiest street in Kyoto, that square, ancient temple town.
Unnoted on government maps or the provost marshal's.
The reason for the latter oversight not the fact that the
Snakepit was off limits to U.S. military personnel (since the

PM delighted in pinpointing unapproved places, a Travelers'
Aid for the uniformed), but largely because it was invisible.
There is no quarreling with something that isn't there. The
Pit was off limits only insofar as it was not on limits. The
proprietress looked upon the act of obtaining a license,
bruiting about what she had to sell and whom she sold it to,
as neither *gentil* nor necessary. Hers was a sin of omission.
But in spite of the relative propriety of such sins, no one is
saying that the whereabouts of the Snakepit was unknown
to the military police. No one makes this claim, but MPs
are people too, with off-duty time, and the management
did not discriminate along occupational lines (although even
at this late date a search might turn up a Negro MP or
two who would dispute this point as a matter of pride).
Their rounds embraced licensed bars, hotels, and cabarets
(including those temporarily out of grace due to a fight or
a traced case of the clap), with occasional forays accompanied by Japanese policemen into the indigenous red-light
areas, where a few jaded or reckless could always be found;
but the MP could expect no reward for rising above the
call of duty and raiding a place that barely existed. The Pit
was unmolested, self-effacing, unseen, and undamned.

Again, location: in the minds, hearts, and jockey shorts
of its clientele, and selected employees. The fronting fruit
store lost in a welter of coffee houses, souvenir shops, drug
and department stores, cinemas, pawnbrokers, trolley stops
and wires, tiny bars along alleys veering off the main street,
the due east mountain vista dotted by temples. Of all the
fruit stands on that thousand-year-old street, the one closest
to the river.

Decor: the ideal Japanese home. Sliding doors, straw
mats, space, a scroll or two, much as in the photographs and
prefabs that make their broadening way across the ocean.

The mats a bit frayed compared to the ones we see, the holes
in the sliding doors or their oilpaper patches a little larger
than life, the w.c. impossible not to locate, in the dark, with
a bad cold; a trap in time of fire, a frozen hell five months
of the year. Two-storied, and on the second a begrudging
concession to the imputed taste of the clientele, a "Western-
style lounge," serving also as bar, with tables and chairs.
Tucked in the corner an organ, Madam's legacy from an
otherwise unsuccessful marriage, decorative but also play-
able, as the enterprising and bored discovered while waiting or drinking a beer. Above the couch a lithograph of
disputed origin depicting a naked cherub with a wand moving toward a glowing cross, upper left, possibly receding.
The one inventoried Pit item, except for her employer,
which Kimiko admitted had been around as long as she had.
And with this mention of Helen (although the Pit remains
unevoked, unreal as ever), it becomes unjust to keep her
from her tale.

When he had neither appeared nor phoned by seven-
thirty, I decided to make other plans. The sporadic action
under way since three in the afternoon showed signs of in-
creasing, although it was still almost entirely a short-time
crowd. I had been awaiting Sixstripes in Maachan's room,
first floor rear, two rooms from the entrance, but could
see them come and go through the gaps in the sliding doors.
From time to time Maachan wandered in from the second-
floor waiting room to rest, or fetch a beer, and gave me her
hungry look, but did not feel it politic to say anything. She
is aware of my dislike for the short-time customer, and
although short-handed (which is why she had to navigate
the stairs herself, keeping the boys content until the girls
were disengaged), it was not yet so bad that she had to press

me into service as a waitress. We both knew that sooner
or later I would be obliged to offer help rather than sit on
my butt in the back room all night, or even until the all-
nighters began to arrive, from roughly nine o'clock. I toyed
briefly with the idea of taking the evening off and going to
a movie, returning in time for the serious-minded people,
but I usually become lonesome in the movies, accompanied
or alone; and, Blakesan, I tell you this because I tell you
everything, I could not face the prospect of sitting with my
Saturday-afternoon permanent for two hours in the dark.
So I could go for a walk in the early Fourth Moon evening
and be free and conspicuous at the same time. But again, let
me be frank. A payday Saturday night. For just the second
time in eight months I found myself unburdened by the
moneyed, aging, far-from-lecher and a tepid liaison which
had Maachan's approval and believe this or not (but it's
true) I felt a well-qualified but quite real sense of excitement when I thought of the unwinding of the long, liquid
evening, the frequent minor and occasionally major crises
calling for wit, diplomacy, and possibly judo (which I
learned, as a girl, during the war); I had been out of it for
so long on this night of nights (although I did not think I
had missed it) that what I felt now could only be called
anticipation—for a sad, wet amalgam which never looks
so futile, even to me, as it does on Sunday morning. What
other conclusion, if one must be drawn (my forebears spin
wildly in their graves): I was born to be a whore.

To fathom the reference to her agitated ancestors we
must turn back the clock some eight hundred years and
come out on a (let us say) bleak, cold day in the Kyoto
area, in the midst of the Taira clan. They ruled supreme
in the middle of the twelfth century, to be crushed and

scattered by the Minamoto near its close. Now, the Taira were easily as corrupt, sentimental, heroic, and brave as their conquerors, as most accounts confirm, and the decisive battle at Dannoura might have gone the other way, so that as we peer down the halls of history we find that if we care to praise the Minamoto we have got to praise the Taira, too; and Helen was as proud of her direct descent from the vanquished as she would have been had Yoritomo been her sire, the man who led the Minamoto to their victory. Prouder, perhaps—defeat sits well on some brows, you know; simpler to explain and explaining more than victory. It was the Taira, loyal, courageous to the last, and when all was lost retiring to the west, finding a new adversary in defeat, wresting subsistence from the soil, taking to farming as they took to war, that gave Helen pride; and whom she feared by remarks and her karma to offend.

But the die was cast. I would remain at the Pit and become reacquainted with what passes in some circles for night life. The next time Maachan came in I said it seemed the sergeant had found something else to do, and I offered to take over her social duties in the bar. She agreed at once, knowing I knew she hoped I would weaken, through drink perhaps, and help out more directly with the short-time crowd—but we knew each other well, and none of this fencing had much effect on our mutual affection. I know you'll demur, Blakesan, but Maachan is an excellent woman in spite of her line of business and a concomitant covetousness, and we have always had something of a mother–eldest daughter relationship. So I fixed my lipstick and went upstairs.

One of the three guests I knew intimately, a corporal from Camp Asakusa; the other two were strangers. The corporal is a comedian: when he woke before I did one morning, he took my favorite shall I say brassière, and did not return it until his next visit, which was nearly three weeks later. There's humor in the theft, had he been a witness to my consternation; but I fail to fathom the joy in jokes which find their perpetrator elsewhere. In any event it was he who greeted me as I came into the room:

"Hey, Lola, your tits are on crooked"—a remark I guessed to be untrue, but I checked them anyway. This evoked laughter, appreciative glances, and an order for three more beers, which Sally was sent to fill by the nice-looking blond boy who sat beside her on the couch and was in the midst of a trial run, to judge by the position of her skirt, which was well above her fat knees. This is Sally's idea of being a hostess, although one must make allowance for her bucolic background, and it is certainly true that the demarcation line in a place like the Snakepit is hazy, unless one goes out of her way to make it clear. It occurred to me I might have to do just that, were one or the other of the pair I didn't know to take it into his head to hire me on a part-time basis. The corporal could vouch for my habits, did they misinterpret these in personal terms, but he could hardly be counted on. Sally returned with the beer, which was kept downstairs in Maachan's icebox.

Things went smoothly for the next half-hour; while I know they had been rowdy before, I brought with me an infectious decorum: we discussed the weather, we were gathered now in a drawing room. Only the sometimes audible exit of a satisfied customer from a nearby room threatened the atmosphere; then the boy on the couch slid his hand along Sally's thigh and his companion eyed me speculatively from the armchair as I leaned, sipping my drink, leading the talk, against the organ. The corporal, unnaturally quiet, had a bottle of Suntory whisky, pouring from it at intervals into his beer, and I began to suspect he had plans for me. He is hornier when drunk, as he knows, and it seemed to me that he was deliberately drinking to excess this early in the evening both to quicken desire and deaden horror at his prodigality, for he was not one to spend money foolishly (cold sober), even on a payday Saturday night—all preparatory, in other words, to inviting me to bed at the preposterous hour of eight p.m., knowing he could probably get the same goods, or a facsimile, at a fraction of the price from ten-thirty on. But he did not want a facsimile—and rather than risk losing me to someone less cautious than himself, he was rapidly becoming that someone, and Sally padded up and down the stairs for more beer. Does this flatter me? I know my capabilities and my customers. And I think it indicative that the two others, although short-time people, made no move to leave the room nor in fact took their eyes off me even after more earthy entertainment became available (and Sally was there all the time); I don't wish to labor the point, Blakesan, but I look upon hostess as the perfect avocation.

The situation reached no denouement. Four new, exuberant arrivals came up the stairs and into the waiting room, trampling under the gossamer thread we have watched unwind. This, in my opinion, is why nothing really dramatic happens in a whorehouse: someone is always coming in. Herding in the newcomers was Maachan herself, who saw them more or less comfortably seated in the small room and beckoned me outside.

"Excuse me, Tomikosan . . ." she said—upon the death of my father last year she became the only person apart from yourself to know and use my given name; some of the girls may have heard her do so, but they know better than to take the same liberty. We do not, my name and I, move in the same circles—". . . but Pop is downstairs and he says he wants to talk to you."

At first the identity of "Pop" escaped me, and I thought she might mean Sixstripes, who had made it after all; but a thumbnail sketch on the way downstairs placed him for me before we reached the first floor. I had not seen him in about six months, so naturally had forgotten him; assumed, if anything, he had been sent home, or found another, or drunk himself to death. I'd be hard pressed to keep simultaneous and fresh the names and faces of my countless friends. Which is not to say that the moment I had the name conjoined with the face, the moment I withdrew the entry "Pop" from the card file of my memory, I did not know the content of every moment we had spent together; I knew this and could also, within a week, tell him the last time he had brought his custom to the Pit. Which I later had the opportunity to do.

Pop was past forty, a career soldier of course (although once more a PFC), rather young-looking beneath the gray crewcut, behind the rimless glasses, and generally pleasant and unassuming. When we reached the bottom of the stairway he was in the act of stuffing his shoes into the remotest corner of the shelves, a practice which stemmed from a series of unfortunate incidents right after he reached Japan, when he woke up three mornings shoeless in three different hotels. This is not a common occurrence in the average hotel nor even in the average whorehouse, which it is safe to assume Pop had euphemistically in mind; but he swears it happened, and has thereafter made certain, regardless of how drunk he might be, that other shoes are more readily available and more attractively lighted than his.

I gave Pop my mischievous and only smile.

"Hello, Helen," he said, and lurched against the AWOL bag which sat limply at his feet. It clanked slightly. Maachan left us immediately to our own devices.

"Long time no see," I said.

"That's right." But it was easy to see he was not geared to amenities. He had a certain haggard look. "Let's go upstairs."

"Upstair very crowded," I said. "Many people in bar. You want to talk, better talk here."

"Let's go to a room then. You busy tonight?"

"Not busy," I said, "if you no want short-time." I did not think he did, to judge from his past behavior and the general data on men his age, who are inclined to spend the night, if only because of the energy lost in removing and putting on their clothes in a short space of time. But I thought it best to make sure. He rallied slightly and reproached me: "Goddamn it, Helen, you know me better than that. Have I ever gone for a short-time before? All through the night is what I got in mind. What is all this Akadama wine for?" He kicked the bag. "I seek companionship. How much for all night?"

"Five thousand," I said, "because early on."

"A hell of a lot," he said. "But I got it."

I led him upstairs to a vacant room, passing the lounge on the way. He paid me, then lay on his stomach across the bed and began to remove the wine bottles from the bag and arrange them in a triangle on the floor. I slipped outside to give four thousand yen to Maachan. The waiting room was nearly empty. All but one of the four newcomers had opted against the social graces (as is natural without a skilled hostess to set the example), taken their drinks into the rooms labeled *Sally, Jane, Peggy, Anna, Joyce* in search of hidden pleasures. (These names were automatically con-

ferred upon the girls by whom the rooms were occupied; Sally remained Sally for the duration of her employ, plied her trade exclusively in "Sally's" room; but her successor, whatever her feelings in the matter, would be called Sally too. It is perhaps some small measure of my standing that my room bore no name; there were in fact three such rooms, all at my disposal.) The one exception was in earnest conversation with the corporal (whose two companions had also vanished) concerning the relative merits of their two battalions, both of which had seen action during the Korean War, although neither had been on the scene. The corporal hailed me as I went by. "Hey, Lola, where you been? I been waitin' for you," aware, I could tell by his tone, that he had waited a bit too long. "Have busy," I said pleasantly. "No can stay."

"Busy hell," the corporal said, twisting around in his chair. Red streamlets fed the green pools of his eyes. "I was here first, wasn't I?"

"Before he telephone," I lied. "Must have appointment payday Saturday night." Which was substantially true, at least so far as I was concerned. My Saturday nights were consigned to Sixstripes, and by appointment.

"That's a line of shit," he said, but not caring, even if it were true; nevertheless subsiding into the chair, the alcohol temporarily checking his determination. "Get me another beer," he said, wheeling round again—maybe wanting one, maybe anxious to keep me there as long as possible. I was on my way downstairs with the money and it was no particular effort to relay the request to Maachan. On the way back I slipped quickly and quietly past the waiting room.

Pop had removed his khakis as well as the apex of the triangle, and was sitting on the bed in his drawers with a

half-full bottle of port. He looked healthier than he had
downstairs, which cheered me. It was likely that the very
elixir which restored the glow of health would eventually
diminish his vigor, but this was an unavoidable risk, since
nothing I might have said or done could curtail his intake
anyway. Pop was a wino, by his own not admission but
observation made with pride, and at his invitation (and since
I could not beat him) I joined him, picking up a bottle, the
right base of the triangle, and pouring the sweet red stuff
into a glass on the night table, Then I put out the overhead
light and switched on the small lamp behind the pillows. I
sat in the easy chair, where the shadows did interesting
things to my dark-green dress, and crossed my legs and
smiled at Pop and drank my wine.

"When's the last time I was here, Helen?" he said, running
a bony hand over his cropped gray hair.

"You no come six months," I said. "Last time you come
Columbus Day. I think rain that night," I added, but that,
of course, was a fiction.

"Damn long time," Pop reflected, and tipped the bottle
once again toward his throat. The wine I was drinking did
not sit well with the beer (which is not a truism, sometimes
it does), and I thought it might be necessary to begin on
the love-making earlier than I had planned. The total out-
lay of energy there sweeps before it such competing interests as, for example, financial problems, or even physical
discomfort—a young sergeant on R & R occupied my at-
tentions for twelve hours running one winter night, to
leave the following morning in an ambulance with an ap-
pendix that had certainly ruptured some time before. With
this in mind, I slipped the dress over my head and came
and sat beside Pop, who once more studied the no longer
symmetrical design, rapping an empty bottle against his

palm. I placed my hand on his thigh, below the tight white
line of the shorts, gripping it slightly to fight off a rush of
dizziness. The beer and wine disputed some no man's land
in the hollow of my belly. Pop patted my hand absently,
made his choice, and tore at the tin foil of a new bottle. I
felt a touch of panic; perhaps I had not taken him literally
enough when he said he had come for companionship. Perhaps he had paid five thousand yen for a drinking friend;
even without the need to actively combat my discomfort,
this would have left me considerably put out since I take
pride, as you know, in behaving consonantly with the time
and place—in bed as well as in the Pit's equivalent of the
salon. In my distress I compounded the error: when he
patted my hand in that fatherly fashion I asked how he
had been filling his off-duty time between visits to the Pit.
And he commenced to tell me, in some detail, while my
stomach did strange things, and I longed to push this old
man back among the pillows.

"You know what I done, Helen, I got tired of cattin'
around, I got me a house and a girl and I settled down. I
met her right outside the camp, a small, sweet thing except
every time she opens her mouth she sounds like a sergeant.
She already had a house so I cased it, we made a deal, and
I moved right in. Her last shack was a first john, he left her
with all but a TV set. For seventy a month I now have a
fine place to lay my body, a place to drink superior to the
bars and barracks, and a place to get my gun off if you follow me. As I say, she's a looker, and I know she is used to
more than seventy a month. But I figure like this: if she
can manage on the sly, not use the house, not pick up anything, and be there when I am, I make no complaints. I
pretty near tell her as much. So things chug along. Then
one day last week, workin' the swing shift five p.m. to mid-

night, the major drops by. He looks over my shoulder. 'Travers,' he says. 'You are punching the wrong keys. Look here—your machine is not even sending. You stink of wine. My wife had a baby girl this afternoon. Here's a cigar. Now go back to bed before I court-martial you.' So at ten o'clock I'm loose and I start downtown for a drink. Then I remember all the wine in the shack and I go there instead. And what do you think I find?"

"She catch other boy," I said, speeding him along.

"Goddamn right she do. She catch mess sergeant. Well, he don't want no trouble, and I don't want no trouble. So he gets dressed and gets out. The girl starts yelling about the MPs if I'm fixing to mess her up. I say, I'm not going to mess her up. All I wanted was a little peace. All I got against her is I catch her at it, which is more than a man has to stand.

"It lasted four months. Pop Travers tries the quiet life. For two months I been cooling it. And now, I return to the Pit, where the joy of domestic bliss is free and clear of the crud of domestic strife!" he concluded, and took a long emptying pull on this second bottle, and to my surprise (for I had assumed that he would shoot his wad by way of his mouth—he said much more than I give you here—that this purge would suffice and he would now pass out. Although the pangs had lessened and my head had cleared, the context created by the bed lamp and removal of my dress was too strong to be quickly dispelled, besides which I was not tired; had he done this I would have had to go outside in search of excitement—perhaps the corporal remained uncommitted, or something else had turned up—and, incidentally, make a little extra money for Maachan and myself, catch an overpriced short-time after all, although money was not the primary impetus), to my surprise he reached out suddenly, put out the bed lamp (that was his style), removed my drawers and his own in what was almost the same motion, and to my great satisfaction set about proving that fortyish PFCs have emphatically not reached the end of the road but can go as hard and as long as they care to, longer probably, the retarding effect of the alcohol. At the conclusion I felt fulfilled, suddenly blissfully tired, cuddled up close to Pop (who had dropped off at once) and fell asleep.

But I dreamed the wild dreams. I dreamt that the giant Buddha at Nara had Rickey's face, while retaining its blank, almond eyes. I dreamt as well, I am sorry to say, that this same Buddha possessed an organ all in keeping with its size, and appeared anxious (with a friendly smile) to use it as I worshiped there. I screamed my defiance and the great Buddha went back overseas. I dreamt of my father, the year my mother died. You are the last Taira, he said. He hit me twice across the mouth, but Rickey appeared from the kitchen and said that was not the way to treat the woman he had asked to be his wife. I said (in a vernacular I have acquired since), Keep your cruddy nose out of affairs between my father and me. He then resorted to force, tried to drag me to a foreign land, but he failed in this, desisted, and took my cherry away. I wandered into the PX, where I had my first job after school, but it was after closing and Rickey came in to buy some toothpaste, as he had the day we met. He conducted this transaction in the dark, his eyes were bright slits, he said he wanted nothing from me any more. Helen, he said, you will never die. Atone, live forever. *Live in a whorehouse forever.* Then he was not Rickey but the Nara Buddha, extending in the PX darkness its great black hand . . . and I screamed.

And woke myself with it, or Maachan, who stood there,

brought me to, keeping her hands on my shoulders, then putting a finger to her lips and beckoning me outside. I shook the sleep and terror from my eyes and looked over at Pop. He had his face to the wall, hunched like a giant fetus, making a soft snoring sound. I slipped on a robe and stepped into the corridor.

"You were having an unpleasant dream?"

"What time is it?" I said.

"Eleven-thirty. Tomichan, listen. I need your help. It's that friend of yours."

"What friend?" I said irritably.

"The one who stole your falsies."

"Is he still here?"

"He left after you went to bed, but he came back about twenty minutes ago. He's incredibly drunk, I could only quiet him down by promising I'd talk it over with you."

"What does he want?"

"To sleep with 'Lola.' All night. He says it's got to be all night. If not he'll 'tear down this paper house.' Tomichan, what shall we do?"

"Doesn't he know I've got a customer?"

"He says it doesn't matter. He says he knows you're not a virgin. He says if I'm not back in five minutes, he's coming up."

"Where is he?"

"In my room. I had to keep him out of the way."

I pulled the sash tight and started down the stairs. He was sprawled on the floor in Maachan's room, his head on a cushion meant for his rear. He sat up quickly when I came in. "Lola, baby," he said, with much maudlin affection. "I been waitin' and waitin' and I thought you wasn't gonna come. How've you been? Don't give me any shit," abruptly shifting gears. "If I don't stay with you tonight no one else does either. So go clean yourself up and let's make whoopee. Six thousand," he said, over my shoulder to Maachan. " 'Sa lot of loot, granma." Which it was. I knew then she would have woken me anyway, had he not been committed to mayhem.

"I no can do, she have to say," Maachan said. It was a truth of sorts. *I* said yes or no. But if he did some damage, I'd be saddled in Maachan's books (and in my own) with the responsibility, a high price to pay. It's not possible for us to summon the MPs at such a time, as another place might, for reasons of which you are aware.

"Already I have customer," I said.

He grinned. "I know. I ain't proud. Let's you and me make a deal and never tell him about it."

"Maybe he wake up," I said.

"So I'll break his ass. No sweat there. Come on upstairs."

"We no want trouble here," I said, and Maachan mumbled assent behind me, although I sensed her concern that I might talk him out of it.

"Nobody wants trouble," he said. "That's human nature. You know me, Lola, a few kicks, but no troublemaker. Your friend don't work tomorrow, Sunday, right? He don't have no reveille to make, right?"

I said I didn't know, but that this was probably true.

"Well, look, I gotta be out by six-thirty. MPs work all the damn time. So you wake me at six, we pitch a little woo, I'm out by six-twenty, you return to your friend who all this time is sleeping like a baby. See?" Again the abrupt transition: "If not, I start in this little room here, and I tear this place apart."

From Maachan, a sharp intake of breath. My duty was clear. Apart from this, Blakesan, I was intrigued by the idea. When my prejudice against the short-time customer was less pronounced, I naturally engaged a handful of clients in the course of an evening; but never had I slept with a pair each of whom expected and deserved my attention all through the night. I have heard of it being done, in fact more neatly still, with neither of the males remotely aware of the other, but it has not happened to me, nor to anyone I know. In addition, the corporal's argument seemed sound: Pop, sleeping the sleep of the wino, would probably not wake until woken, certainly not at the ungodly hour of six o'clock. I could be back sharing his bed, if not embrace, catch up on the sleep I would certainly need, and he be none the wiser.

So there it was. I took his hand. It was on the floor above the second, the termination of the stairway, more an attic than anything else, the room we reserved for officers, troublemakers, and other offbeat people, the one chance for the "Sallys, Margies. Janes" to leave their labeled cloisters. The ceiling, actually the roof of the house, was abnormally low, and I cautioned him, though a knock on the head would not have meant much anyway. He had no firm grasp of where he ended and the world began, and one of his first moves after lying down was to put his hand through the window situated above the bed. It did not face the street; it overlooked a high, narrow enclosure which served as kitchen for the Pit and the owners of the fruit store, who lived in the next house, and fortunately no one was there at this hour. A draft streamed through the broken pane. I felt the cough rising; I dove beneath the covers, at which the corporal bestirred himself, removed his clothes, and did the same. But I was too late. It came and wracked me for a quarter of an hour.

"Loll, you got TB," he said, leaning over and placing his mouth where it would have the happiest effect on this disease.

"Never happen!" I said sharply, since it happened to be true.

The corporal followed the script, engaged me once in that venerable combat (a far briefer, less satisfactory encounter than the one with Pop had been), then rolled over and went to sleep. I found it no great problem to follow suit. I was deathly tired.

What happened to him clearly was the great dry awakening which often follows a drunken sleep: the liquor wears off and you find yourself staring and sober in a dark room hours before it makes sense to be awake—perhaps you've experienced it yourself, Blakesan, you're not a stranger to alcohol; in his case, however, he could not have had more than another hour's sleep at best, and the tragedy was further diminished by the proximity of entertainment. So for the second time (if I had not screamed myself awake the first), I woke to hands on my shoulders and with favors to bestow. The corporal realized his desire with what was, for me, a minimum of cooperation, then went down to the w.c. I tried to sleep; sleep was an evil, gaping hole, from which I pulled back each time, just in time. After what must have been an hour I saw through slitted eyes dawn filter through the skylight, and the corporal, who had amused himself since his return by a mumbled medley of talk and song, suddenly fell quiet and as noiselessly as he could manage slipped from the bed and began putting on his clothes. I was puzzled by this seeming concern on the part of one who showed so few qualms about waking me (then keeping me awake) a short time before—until I remembered that my time was not this prankster's, this devotee of the

joke he would not be there to enjoy, but Pop's, trustfully
sleeping on the floor below, and I sat up quickly and groped
in the bedclothes for my pants.

The corporal seemed suprised. "Where you goin', Lola?
You don't have to get up yet. It ain't even six. You better
get some sleep."

"Shit."

"Now, is that the way to begin Sunday morning? You'll
be bitchy all day without your beauty sleep."

"I have customer," I said, locating and slipping into my
drawers.

"So early in the morning? Don't you ever get no rest?"

I made no reply.

"You mean the fella from last night. By God, I almost
forgot about him. Yeah, you better get right down there.
Funny it slipped my memory."

"Maybe you forget also you break window last night?"

"What window?"

I pointed to the shattered pane.

"Now, Loll, I ain't the window-breaking type. I didn't
even know one was there. What the hell's a window doin'
so close to the bed anyway?"

"You pay three hundred yen, enough to fix."

"Ain't I already forked out enough? I didn't break no
window. I think it was the guy downstairs."

I saw that hope of extracting the money was slight, and
perhaps the inconvenience and the one hundred yen to
replace the pane would serve as precept to Maachan, although I doubted this. I walked past him, avoiding his
fingers, down two flights, to the toilet. I came back up to
the second floor and slid back the door. The bed was empty.

He was standing in front of the mirror in his drawers,
buttoning the cuffs of his khaki shirt. He looked noncom-

mittal but the silence was enough; Pop is talky when things go well. At last he said, "Where've you been, Helen?" reaching onto the night table and taking a good-sized gulp from the bottle of port. The room was full of empties, foil, and a number of fulls. I tried to remember how many we'd had the night before; perhaps I could form a rough idea of how long he'd been awake. It proved too complicated. The fact that he asked where I had been told me he had been up long enough to render suspect obvious replies, like down to the bathroom.

"Why you wake up so early? Today Sunday, holiday."

"I go on day shift today. I told you that, didn't I? That's why I come in so early last night. No reveille, but I got to be at work by eight. I told you that."

"No, I think you forget."

"Where've you been, Helen?" He sat on the bed, bottle in hand, much as he had been last night. I knew Pop better than to fear violence, particularly since learning his reaction to a still more serious crisis, in his story the night before. My chief concern was to lie well, thus sparing him anguish.

"I no can sleep last night. No can stay here. I go downstair, talk to Maachan, she no sleep too. We eat, play cards. I think you no get up till late."

He looked at his watch, then back at me. His expression said nothing at all. He upended the bottle, drained it, reached for one of the two still left. I removed the robe and went and sat in the chair.

"I'll tell you how it is, Helen. I'm a reasonable guy. When I pay good money in a place like this I like to get my money's worth, even if all that means is that the girl stays in the same place all night. Now wait, I know you didn't do nothin' on the shady side. All you did was play cards with the old bag, but that ain't the point. The point is you should have been here all night in case I woke up, which I did. I know you wouldn't screw around on my time, but you should of stuck around. Ain't that right?"

I nodded my honest assent.

"Because I'm an old geezer whose main interest is peace and quiet and I might kick off one morning while you're playin' cards and you would be the loser." He beckoned with the bottle. "Now step over here where we can do what you would rather been doin' all night, if I know my Helen."

"You got time?" I asked anxiously.

"For that there's time," he said breezily, and, he in shirt and drawers, we met once more in the gray light and panted and moved until Pop came, an inferior coupling from my point of view, but not bad for Pop. His spirits soared. He graciously conferred, before departure, upon the Pit or me, whichever I preferred, the unused portion of his wealth, the bottle and a half. "Hurry back," I said, and he said he would, as soon as he felt the need for the kind of stimulation we provided.

"From here on in when the spirit moves I'll take my gear down to the Pit, where the pace is slow and Helen gives value." And with that he stepped out onto the landing with his empty bag, waving me back when I offered to see him out. As he pulled shut the sliding door, I caught a glimpse of the corporal, descending from the floor above.

What had delayed him I do not know—perhaps he had been combing the room for something to steal; perhaps, since it was too early for his bus, going through the movie magazines we kept upstairs. Whatever the reason, there he was, moving toward Pop, and I leaped from the bed and pressed against the door.

As you might predict, Blakesan, having read widely among

the fiction of many nations, the two knew each other. I can't say what I expected, or feared, but I hung on every word as they stood and talked, the corporal on the staircase, Pop right outside the door.

"Ryder, ain't no MPs allowed in here."

"Well, bust my britches. A man your age oughta be ashamed. I thought you had a shack, anyway."

"I give it up. I come home to Helen."

"Who's Helen?"

"Sweetest little piece in town. You going back to camp?"

"Uh huh. Listen man, you don't want to say nothing about tail, understand, *not a word*, until you spent a night with Lola, which I'm just comin' from. Now, there is class goods. You ever tried Lola?"

"Never heard of her."

"You been to this place before?"

"Hell, I'm a trustee."

"And you never heard of Lola?"

"Not since I left the Coast. What's she look like?"

"Like a pisscutting witch, if you want to know the truth. But she's got lots of class. Let's get started, the bus is due. What's this Helen chick like?"

"Oh, a little on the light side. But I'm no tit-man anyway."

"They're all that way," the corporal said. Noisy even in stockinged feet, he thumped past my door. Then I heard Pop throw back over his shoulder, "You say this Lola looks like a witch?"

"Yeah, yeah, but not so's you'd mind. You dig, a *good-looking* witch."

And that was all. The rest—that there was more who can doubt—was lost to me around the bend in the staircase.

I could conjecture, or go to bed; before they reached the street I was asleep.

The corporal has been back since, wearing a shiteating grin and parrying attempts to get the whole story. Poor Pop has never returned. I, on my part, have come by a story which rounds out my repertoire, this tale of intrigue during the Fourth Moon; it bristles, I think, with a peculiar significance. Don't you . . ."

Here she burst into a fit of coughing, and we left the park for the warmth of a nearby coffee shop. It stopped after a time, as it would have anyway. Consumption, according to their records, kills no Japanese.

Don't you? Think the Song of Helen pleads to be preserved? That before the Grim Reaper who awaits us all (despite her dreamy fears) comes whirling twirling to part her forever from the throng, or sends her back to the same hectic place with more or less money, there should come a scribe to commit her tune to the rumtumtum of history? I met Kimiko at a poker game on the Left Bank, standing at attention in potter's field, I met her in the midst of a thin book about tea, and we had our little ceremony.

The Nickel Misery of George Washington Carver Brown

THE DAY that Carver Brown fell backward from the freshly painted pinnacle of failure (setting even for him a new low) was the day before Thanksgiving Day: it dawned in frozen reds and blues, without portent. Between the sleep-smelling barracks and the temporary security of the mess hall he was called upon to face three minor crises, indisputable sources of discomfort, but nothing like harbingers because they had all happened to him before. In the crowded latrine his towel disappeared as he groped for it blind, soapy-eyed; back at his bunk his bootlaces had become tightly knotted, his blankets were wet, his mattress on the floor; as (having to repair the damage) the last man

to appear at the reveille formation, he naturally attracted
the attention of Corporal Cherry, who sliced off the open
button of his field-jacket pocket with a straight razor and
ordered him to replace (and button) it before entering the
mess hall. Unstrung as Carver was by all three incidents, he
would not have said that they surprised him. They repre-
sented, at the five-and-one-half-week point, the sum and
definition of his military experience, foreshadowed (on the
day before Thanksgiving) nothing more than the status
quo, another day of continual low-key persecution. Weeks
later, when Carver's mother had keened away the sharper
edges of her grief, she would say that on that day (and
on the three days previous, too) at precisely one-forty in
the afternoon she had felt pass through her back and spine
a murderous unforgettable pain, as if a fat hand had brought
her to a great giddy height and slammed her from it to the
ground, but Carver was possessed of no such (real or
imagined) extrasensory power; received no indication on
Wednesday or at any time previous that his luck had totally
left him until that fractionary instant (and perhaps not even
then) when there was nothing else to believe. The frigid
bloody sun lofted into the cloud-streaked, quickening sky,
the second platoon scattered before the first, third, and fourth
because Wednesday breakfast was their turn to queue up
first outside the mess hall, and Carver Brown, who enjoyed
food, stamped, shuffled, and whined completely in character
into the barracks to hunt in the chaos of his foot-locker
tray for his sewing kit. He had made this early-morning
search a dozen times before.

The second platoon's athletic dash toward breakfast left
still another in its wake, a non-competitor (whom it would
have out-distanced anyway). This was Roger Hines, the
group's least agile man. At the command to fall out he took

a long awkward step out of the first squad and continued toward the barracks, while the trainees jostled and raced behind him to the mess hall. Eating was not foremost in his mind. Copper-tinted and frail, he had a terrible brittle quality, his stooped, skinny form warning *Touch me and break me*, and since the second day of the fourth week, when he tripped while double-timing and twisted his ankle, he existed in a state approaching grace, an accepted member of the so-called fifth platoon. This was the three-man fringe group allowed to straggle to the training areas at its own pace behind the company proper because of leg trouble—a man who had broken both a year ago on an obstacle course and spent most of the time since shuttling between various basic-training units and the post hospital; a man who contracted in the Army (and almost overcame) polio, eighteen months before, and claimed wistfully, in the twilight of his military career, to be awaiting early separation; and most recently Hines, his ankle not now seriously injured nor even when he fell, but its job done, italicizing what his body and bearing should have thundered from the start: that here, in this brittle, silent twenty-six-year-old, was nothing less than a great potential tragedy. Given an hour of crisis and not the slack time following the Korean truce; a sixteen-week infantry training regimen in place of this abbreviated, almost token program for men being groomed for noncombatant duty in the Signal Corps; given, in other words, the military context in which even gratuitous brutality commands an aura of necessity, Hines might conceivably have had it. But he had been drafted at the right time, sent to the right place, come by the right injury, and his luck was going to hold.

Only Brown was in the barracks as Hines hobbled down the center aisle: Brown sitting on his bunk and sewing with

a frantic clumsiness, still wearing the jacket, mumbling furious regional epithets about the character of Corporal Cherry
that might have offended Hines at a less urgent time.
Brown's presence alone was enough to disturb him, yet he
knew he would be lucky to have to cope with no other dis-
tractions: the handful of trainees who might give up
their early-breakfast privilege to fuss around their areas or,
worse, use the latrine. His heart pounding under the field
jacket, Hines reached the end of the center aisle without the
barracks door slamming behind him, ducked with his rifle
into the empty latrine, placed the weapon between the wall
and his commode, and grabbed at the buckle of his pants.
For roughly twenty seconds he defeated himself by ignoring
the hard-won privacy to concentrate on the prospect of its
imminent dissolution, but he heard no footsteps and the
sound of no door, and Carver's mumbling blended finally
with the troop noises outside and he was on the point of
achieving a kind of success when the saccharine whine broke
into his ear.

"Man, why that mother always pick on me?"

He had not even heard him, neither stop his mumbling
nor approach; he had built up for the first time in seven
miserable weeks the kind of insulation he guessed he would
have to have if he was ever going to learn to manage in what
could at best be a delicate temporary privacy (for it was
mad to expect him to cope with the rushed early-morning
shoulder-to-shoulder public performance, men lined up
heckling, urging haste), and all the insulation had done was
prevent him from composing himself for what he should
have learned by now was the inevitable failure. Because
someone always came in. He would have to wait until tonight, after lights out, and even then until the last diehard

poker players and letter writers were gone from the latrine. He had waited painfully the night before, only to discover that Brown's tormentors were on the prowl: men deferring sleep until Brown crawled noisily beneath his blankets, then yanking him out, smothering his protests, dragging him to the shower room, administering the traditional GI shower. So last night too had been a failure. His insides convoluted strangely, dipped against the sudden shock of Brown's materialization. He felt sick with frustration, carrying a poisonous weight of a thousand pounds. He wished for absolutely nothing now but that he had heard the boy's approach.

"Man, why everbody always pick on me?" Brown repeated. He continued to work on the field jacket, his chin scraping his chest, the low, plump body half in and out of the commode room, his eyes crossed on the needle and thread. "There's three hundred boys in this company, they all screw-ups, why that Cherry and everbody always pick on me?"

Because you're built for guilt, you black fool, Roger thought. He couldn't move to wipe himself.

"Copperhaid, you smart," Carver went on. "Where you from anyhow, New York? You see how they wet my blanket this mornin' after somebody take my towel? How that Cherry pull out that razor before daylight and try to cut off my haid? Why they do that to me, Copperhaid? Why they mess with me instead of you and everbody else?"

"I have no idea," Roger said harshly, in the strident tones he had used all his life as a substitute for communication. Loud and with perfect diction in love, hate, and neutrality. It set off in the latrine the other's soft, accented whine. "And my name isn't Copperhead. It's Hines, Roger B."

Carver glanced behind him in response to the tone, although he was standing with his rump against the wall. "But everbody call you that," he protested. "Ever damn body."

"My name is Hines," Roger said loudly, "and that is the only name I answer to. Any other I've acquired since being in the Army because of the color of my skin I feel privileged to ignore." He would have retracted that; pinned insanely here to an unreal toilet seat by a dumb suffering son of the South, telling him things he could not even bring himself to write home about this nightmarish time, not even to his wife.

Above the fat cheeks Carver's eyes grew wide. His mouth hung slack between laughter and surprise. Abruptly he discarded the suppliant's role for its opposite, and he said, "You's all confused," slipping the needle into his pocket and easing (across from Hines) onto a lidless commode. "You think us boys call you Copperhaid because you a nigrah? Naw, man. You look like a damn snake," Carver said, guffawed suddenly, and doubled over onto himself, the top of his head inches from Roger's knees. And straightened at once, with a look of joy. "It just the way your face sits, man, all tight across the bone like that. The way you don't seem to have no ears. All the blood gone out of your mouth. Nothin' to do with bein' a nigrah, man, you just resembles a snake, that's all. You unnerstan'?" His interest was all directed toward Roger now; he had forgotten himself. "Some boy tells me you from New York, Copperhaid. Where y'all live at, Hahlem?"

And still Hines could not rise; to leave or (better, but a dream) collect the power in one hundred thirty pounds and smash this fat-cheeked, persecuted, black-faced boy: this was the court fool, the butt, the door mat of the company, baiting him, Hines, one of the few who left him alone while

hating him with a ferocity his tormentors could never muster—this was his *worst enemy* sitting there grinning fully
clothed on a toilet seat touching-distance away, not even
dimly aware that he flirted with what would never become
disaster. It was almost too much to bear.

"Why . . . don't . . . you . . . get . . . some . . .
breakfast," Hines said, and again Brown felt tempted to look
over his shoulder to see who Copperhead was talking to.

"Plenty of time," Carver said. "If I can't be in there first,
I just as quick be last. That way Copul Cherry maybe be
out and I don't have so much worryin' to do. You live in
that Hahlem, man?"

"My home is in Syracuse," Hines said.

"Where that at? A boy tell me you go to *college* up
North. That right, man?"

"Yes!" Hines almost shouted. *Where I learned what I was
born to fear and hate and hoped to God would never meet
except where I had to every day in my own spoiled insides.*
Two trainees, through with breakfast, walked into the wash-
room. Despair made him brave, and he grabbed at the toilet
paper. The situation could only grow worse, and he would
rise.

Suddenly Carver began to whine once more, leaning toward him:

"Then you must be pretty smart, Copperhaid. Maybe
you can say why everbody in this here company pick on
Georgia Brown?"

"Because you like it and you want them to," Roger said,
and stood jerkily and trembling and looked straight ahead
at the bare wall over Carver's clipped round head and pulled
up and buckled his pants. He reached for his rifle and limped
out hurriedly, not stopping to wash his hands. But it came
anyway (as he had magically known it would), Brown's

voice, reaching after and transfixing him, nailing him to
his own cross a foot or two from freedom:

"*Damn*, Copperhaid, if you ain't just buttoned up the
longest sonbitch I ever seen."

Only Cherry, Sergeant Braun, and Mentor, the mess sergeant, were at the cadre table when Brown sidled in at
the door. Cherry sat at the end of the table, facing the entrance, Braun to his right. Mentor was opposite Cherry, his
back to the door. Brown looked over warily, but the corporal's big-jawed face was down into his coffee mug. Brown
took a step toward the table anyway, then changed his mind,
reached for a tray, and went over to the serving line. Sergeant Braun glanced at Cherry, but he didn't have to. Cherry
waited until the second man had two strips of fatty bacon
suspended over Carver's tray.

"Brown!"

The boy wheeled and the fried eggs leaped from his tray
and skittered along the floor. "Aww!" Carver said.

The mess sergeant spun around on the bench. "Goddamn,"
he said. "*God*damn. And here we just got through workin'
our tails to the bone GI-in' the floor last night. Buddy, you're
going to clean that up, along about now. And eat 'em if
you want to. Because right there are your eggs for this
mornin'. If this ain't the asskissinist bunch of trainees," he
appealed to Braun. "Pick 'em up. Then go on back out and
get a mop," he said to Brown.

"In a minute, Sergeant," Cherry said. "I want him over
here."

"Well, let him pick up the damn eggs before the captain
or somebody comes in and breaks their neck," Mentor said.

"You heard him," Cherry said. But Carver was already
on his knees, trying to coax the eggs (one yolk miraculously

intact) with knife and fork back onto his tray, trying desperately not to compound the damage; succeeding, and only the moist outline and a figure eight of yellow remained on the concrete floor. He approached the cadre mess table with the tray held out in front of him, the edge of it pressing into his belly, and in five seconds his face ran the gamut, a dash, a pinch of everything. He was having trouble (an old problem) in forming an attitude.

Cherry looked up at him. "Now you see," he said gently. "If you had come right over to me like I told you to do at reveille and showed me your button and *then* went about getting your breakfast, you wouldn't have got all shook up and dropped your fried eggs and picked up any extra duty tonight. And I *know* you got better things to do with your time at night than fuss around the mess hall."

"Nobody say nothin' 'bout no extra duty, man," Carver said.

"Brown, when a man eats in the Army, it's a holy time. His mind and body has got to be free and completely at rest. There is positively no one messing with the troops at mealtime. That's how I can guarantee Sergeant Mentor don't mean for you to clean up his floor now, but he would like to see you back here around six o'clock tonight."

"He'll mop that crud up now," Mentor said. "If you send him back here tonight to help out the poor KPs, nobody's kickin'."

"You hear that, Brown? The sergeant has got you both ways. There's no pleasing some people. Suppose you take them dirty eggs out of my face and let me see that button now."

"Copul, I thought I'd clean my rifle tonight," Carver begged. "It's been a long while since I got that mother all stripped down and oiled and all. Y'all remember you had me in the mess hall ever day last week. It's sewed real good, Copul," he said, as Cherry's hand reached ominously for his jacket pocket.

"Well, now, you don't have to be no expert sewer," Cherry said reasonably, lifting the flap and tugging at the button, once. "Just so long as she's nice and tight and always closed. You know me and my razor are getting pretty tired of cutting it off damn near every morning. You ever think of it that way?"

Carver had narrowed it now (a way to feel), the whine doing battle with no more than a tentative gaiety.

"Copul, you ain't got to cut anyhow. If you just go and *tell* Carver 'bout that button, you see how fast I get the mother closed. But the way everbody take on after me in barracks I just don't have time to worry 'bout it. You know what they done last night? They pull me out of baid and give me another GI shower, and they just give one to me day before yesterday. And when I get back to baid, don't you know I'm short-sheeted? And got to strip the sonbitch down and make it up in the dark? And this mornin'. . ."

"All right, young soldier," Braun cut in. "You get that floor cleaned up and put something in your belly. And not stand here pissing and moaning all day. We march out in five minutes."

"Yes suh," Carver said, secure in (warmed by) the knowledge that the field first sergeant was teasing him. Didn't the man's wrist watch, resting face upward on the table, allow twenty minutes before the fall-in whistle blew? "Carver's goin' in half a second to fetch a mop. I just got to make sure that Copul Cherry know that if he sends me out to the kitchen tonight I ain't never goin' to get . . ."

"MOVE OUT!" Braun yelled, half rising, and Carver moved out, whining, on his lips the corpse of a smile.

From the rear of the hall where he lingered over coffee, Tom Frazier watched what (from that remove) was little more than a pantomime, an interracial dumbshow set in motion by Cherry's sharp summons, and closed by Braun's overresonant dismissal, and highlighted by the short (soundless) arc the eggs described on the way to the floor. He had to have a theory if he was not going to be ashamed of the way this type of incident still had the power to amuse him, and over the weeks he had developed one, of a middling complexity, and just possibly true. It held that while Carver Brown was a scapegoat, a Christ-figure, and a clown, he was none of these things because he was a black man. His color had no bearing on the continuous round of double-pronged persecution (in which Frazier—while admitting his interest—played no part); he was simply the unfortunate heir to certain transcendent morbid qualities which made him a convenient receptacle for and a symbol of corporate guilt and suffering.

This was the theory (briefly put) that Frazier had to have. He required it because he was a militant egalitarian; he had become this only recently, against considerable odds, and he would not tolerate his slightest backsliding; not until (later: after the fall) it no longer had to go by that name.

It was not a bad theory, but it took (to Frazier's mind) some shoring up, because he noticed a great deal. He did not miss Brown's field-hand shuffle, his telltale wool, his ridiculous speech; he was even aware of the broad piece of irony staged at reveille two or three times a week by Corporal Cherry, when he brandished his outsized razor (which he had come by earlier in the cycle through confiscation from a since-court-martialed, lithe, violent, altogether unhumorous Negro boy) and slashed at Brown's jacket;

he noticed these things, and he was obliged to dispose of them. The razor was simply the form the persecution took in the hands of someone like Cherry; while no doubt a less subtle bigotry did play a part, as in the case of someone like Griever, a Tennessee mountaineer; but these were merely *effects*, existing (within the larger framework) alongside more congenial evidence: as for example Brown's frequent discomfort at the hands of trainees (and cadre too) who hailed from large cities in the North, or at the hands of the grinning Negro cook out in the kitchen with whom Brown jockeyed, at that moment, for custody of an idle mop, seeming to have almost gained it, to have teased it free, until the cook tired of the game and sent him on principle to fetch one from the mop rack outside—his blackness no more explained Brown's role in Charlie Company than the coloration of the limping Hines accounted for his being spared this kind of misery; it explained, in other words, nothing at all. So Tom Frazier lingered over coffee in the mess hall, and allowed himself to be mildly (but watchfully) amused.

He was a tall, athletic Southerner who had been expelled (as he would later, in part, tell Hines) from a fraternity for being apprehended (during Homecoming Week) hosting a Negress in the fraternity president's bedroom. The expulsion had turned his thinking into strange and unaccustomed channels, but he tracked these channels down tenaciously (with no backsliding) because he had that kind of mind. He was drafted not long after the incident, and, while he professed a strong distaste for military service, he enjoyed having to cope with the challenges and the inconvenience of the six weeks up to here; and he had gained time (and an excellent set of situations) in which to test his fresh convictions. He wished only that he might have been assigned to a Northern camp, but, with luck, this too might come in time.

He was about to leave (Brown was busy mopping the floor, and only Mentor sat at the cadre table now) when Hines walked into the mess hall, removed the helmet liner from his flat, fuzzed top, and reached for a coffee cup. So Frazier put off leaving for a while and watched the snake-faced copper boy limp up the aisle. And tried to draw him with his eyes. But Hines (moving deliberately, almost in slow motion, gentling his brittle, damaged bones) jerked his downcast eyes from table to table and sat down at the first empty one, half the distance between Frazier and the serving line. Frazier stared at the brown tapering fingers as they wormed a cigarette from the field-jacket pocket and trembled in the lighting it, watched Hines inhale with all of his body, suck the smoke deep into the translucency of him, visibly almost into his belly, and then lower his face to the oversized coffee mug and lock his fingers around its bulk; and he decided to try once again to make contact, although he had been rebuffed by the fellow in the six weeks a half-dozen times. He picked up his helmet liner, his empty tray, and he covered the ground from table to table in long rapid strides.

In reaching across his chest for the cigarette, Hines glanced up and collided briefly with the wall of Frazier's eyes. He actually felt their impact; so he lowered his gaze to the flame's kind glare, slitted his eyes for the journey down to the black smoking drink, and told himself that Frazier was not looking at him, could not be, because he had no reason to; that if he was looking at him (if he had a reason), it would probably mean a confrontation, further distress, and he had already (by breakfast) filled his quota for the day. So when he sensed the form beside him, nothing

remained but to gulp the scalding coffee (yet barely diminish it) and burn himself.

"Morning, Hines. Mind if I join you?"

But he was on his feet, the corner of the table knifing between them, Frazier still bulking above him, like an adult
over a child. "I . . . was . . . just . . . leaving," Hines
said.

"Christ, man, you just came in. Why don't you sit tight
and let's chat for a while. Do you make it all right till noon
with only black coffee for a breakfast?"

"I was just leaving," Hines said loudly. "I'm sorry."

"Nothing to be sorry about," Frazier said, but the boy
was already on the move, a wounded quarry, scuttling
down the aisle.

"That old Northern hospitality," Frazier said quietly,
aloud. "Just like you read about. Why I believe we'll con-
verse yet, you unsociable so-and-so," and followed Hines
rapidly to the exit, caught and passed him wordlessly as
somewhere in the half-light Braun's whistle blew shrilly,
three long blasts, beginning the day.

It took anywhere from fifteen to twenty-five days for a
company to learn to the last man of Corporal Cherry's
unique means of supplementing his income, a group alert-
ness determining the interval, *esprit de corps*, and the sound-
ness of communication lines. He was circumspect, and taci-
turn, and there was nothing public about the money-making
situation, although at first glance the opposite seemed true.
The three-hundred-odd men lay in neat rows on their backs
in the training area, each engrossed in the taut private world
of the particular exercise, regarding fixedly (depending on
their stamina, the angle's acuteness) toes, crotch, or sky,
and the nature of Cherry's activity in an exerciser's imme-

diate vicinity was not (at first) carefully observed, even by the object of such attention. A man could not help but be aware (although L-shaped, concentrating) of the looming presence of a member of the cadre, and when Cherry bent to him he expected his position to be manually adjusted, or at least to be reprimanded; Cherry would occasionally accommodate, but more often he straightened in silence, leaving the trainee bewildered until the end of the exercise when the man stood, dusted himself off, and reached to the ground for his ID tag and keys—and nothing more. By the time even the most alert group discovered (to the last man) the most effective means of coping with the corporal (you left your change in the barracks, in your foot locker), he had added to a given month's pay check between twenty and thirty dollars.

The group of which Carver Brown was a member adhered to the norm in this respect, contributed twenty-seven dollars in small denominations over the first twelve working days and then abruptly wised up, much more rapidly than they should have, almost as if someone had hung a notice on the company bulletin board, *You will bring no change out onto the training field*. Although a cycle rarely yielded more than (even as much as) this one had, it had never done so quite so fast, and the complete, sudden stoppage left Cherry disgruntled and mystified. But, the Army being what it was, he had no recourse but silence.

Cherry had taken a bullet in the left buttock in Korea, not far from his spine, had emerged from the well-intentioned but necessarily imperfect medical setup somewhere behind the lines with a slight permanent limp which rendered him unfit for further combat duty but did not otherwise inconvenience him, and he had been sent to fill the niche of shaper-of-men at the basic-training camp. The life suited him. Disappointments, like the present one, were rare, and more serious irritations rarer still. There had been the need to scrub down the barracks after the last cycle because the captain had been dissatisfied with the departed trainees' cleaning job, and had held the cadre responsible —but this was just. Cherry (a corporal with a combat record) had not relished the work—cleaning and mopping up after these men who were something even less than subordinates, a race apart—but he had not questioned its equity. It would teach the cadre not to make the same mistake next time. (He had not made the mistake at all—his building was the only one of the four which had passed inspection, but the captain ordered him in to work with the others, mentioning collective responsibility.) If these gold-bricking weak-kneed civilian people headed for the Signal Corps thought they had it made for these eight weeks as well as the time after, they were probably right—but they would not have it as made as they thought. He had seen to that through the two and one-half cycles up to here, and, after the recent mandatory housecleaning, the rest of the noncoms would probably see to it too. Cherry disliked none of the trainees so much as the idea of them, the knowledge of what they were going out into (and what not) and he treated them all with the same impartiality, except when a man begged for, demanded the only kind of attention he had to give, as had Brown. Even here, he enjoyed Brown, he had nothing personally against Brown. Cherry hated no man.

Yet that Wednesday morning he was to come close to it, striding through the ranks of L-shaped men, straightening buckling legs and barking commands, believing himself reconciled by now, the sixth week, to the empty pockets and the bare earth, but learning in an instant how wrong he was as somewhere behind him the coins jingled, clattered, and kept coming with jack-pot regularity; he spun to the sound and witnessed the end of it, the last few striking the clay surface and wobbling away from the rest, the stumpy boy turning his head on its cushion of interlaced fingers and uttering a noise of anguish—Brown. A lame cat, he glided over a straining form as the instructor called, "Keep it going, five more reps now, one-two-three-four," met Brown's shocked, pleading eye for only the time this took, bent to scoop before the exercise ended, and stopped, half-way down.

Pennies lay by Brown. Copper and silver ones, dull ones and shining; some rolling still but most piled neatly in the shadow of his thigh, a modest hill of money, pennies. Terrified and silent, Brown implored from his place on the ground, his fingers twitching beneath his head, his eyes wide, his body still. Cherry straightened empty-handed, and the flush crept upward from his jaw.

"Brown, you son of a bitch. . ."

From the platform came the command to rise. Carver struggled to his feet with all the rest, but "Attention!" was too much to ask: his chin inched forward onto his chest, his eyes struggled to focus on the pile. Cherry kicked it then. He dug the boot of his good leg into the heart of the mound and sent the money flying as from the platform came the command, "Rest!" and Brown with a wild look started to sink to the ground.

"Stand up!" Cherry screamed.

"Copul, that my *money* there you . . ."

"I said stand up! Does this here look like the PX? You see something out here you going to buy?"

"Copul, that fifty cent I got till payday, why you kick it that way, man?"

"Don't 'man' me, buddy," Cherry said furiously; "I want to know if you think there's something *humorous* in bringing fifty pennies out here?" seeking the source of his anger, to explain it by unmasking malicious intent, although he knew the boy would not dare. "Every goddamn body else seems to know we leave our money in the barracks when we go out to train. You need an engraved invitation?"

"Copul, listen. Lemme tell you why. I was in the haid this mornin' talkin' to Copperhaid—y'all know who Copperhaid is, that skinny nigrah boy—and when I come back out to my area, some of the boys has took off with my two locks and I can't even close up my uniforms and my foot locker neither, and all I could carry was my money, so I took it along out here. I know some of the boys talk in the barracks about some cadreman he take all your money if you lose it out here, but it wasn't safe noplace else. I can't even get no toothpaste till payday, Copul Cherry."

"Somebody took your locks?"

"Sure did, Copul," Carver said.

"If you'd had them lockers locked, that couldn't have happened now, could it?"

"Naw, suh. But I had to open them mothers for my sewin' kit."

"Well, now, that's pretty much toughtit. Brown, you didn't bring those lousy pennies out here just to piss me off, did you?"

"Naw, Copul."

"I seem to be pissed off anyway, don't I. And I'm thinking if it gets any worse you'll be in the kitchen on extra detail every day until the end of the cycle, and never smell another week-end pass."

"Copul Cherry, excuse me, but I ain't never been on pass yet. They always askin' me one of the genul orders 'fore they give one to me, and them genul orders too long for Carver to remember. Y'all had me on extra duty ever Saturday since basic began, anyway. If I can just get my hands on that fifty cent . . ."

"Brown, you listen to me. You're the lowest form of gold-bricking excuse for a soldier I have ever seen in all my time. If you bend for one—not fifty but one—of those goddamn coins you're going to be working a twenty-hour day from here to the end and everything up to now will seem like a Sunday picnic. You'll hope you were dead, you know what I mean? Now drop to the ground and do your pushups like the rest of these gold-bricks and *remember what I said,*" and kicked at a coin in reach and turned away in disgust; the fat, perspiring, active face seemed an inch away from tears. Or was it joy?

Pennies! He limped away furiously while Carver quivered in self-pity and indignation, thinking *If I don't have money I might as well be daid* (but knowing better than to scrabble behind Cherry's back or even snatch at the coin or two within reach). *Why that mother always got to pick on me.*

Sergeant First Class William Divino, a thirty-year-old combat veteran, awoke in high spirits on the day before Thanksgiving and retained this feeling throughout the sluggish, workday morning, which did not necessarily imply the top-level functioning of his creative powers. In fact, the opposite might have been true: it took him, in high spirits, almost three hours to hammer out and smooth the doggerel he would probably have hammered out and smoothed, feeling down at the mouth, in half that time, so that not until the class on booby traps and mines, the lesson in squad tactics, the chaplain's assault on pornography were all history did he feel ready to commit to public performance and scrutiny the verses inspired by the event he had witnessed (strolling a rank or two behind) some three hours before. The event itself might have damaged the good feeling (hastening thereby its own commemoration), but today it did not. While there was no gainsaying the need for it, there was no speeding up the song. With the ready-made melodies frozen into perpetuity more through the demands of folklore than military need, or desire, Sergeant Divino marched his third platoon homeward for the noon break, a cooperative, hungry bunch, suited at least as well for choral work as soldiering, responding heartily to his alternating bass and falsetto, the greatest quantity of sound issuing from the five or ten who had been eyewitnesses, the trainees who could boast that they were there:

"There's pennies all over the field,"   "YOU'RE RIGHT!"
"There's pennies all over the field,"   "YOU'RE RIGHT!"
"Pick 'em up,"   "ONE TWO!"
"Pi-ick 'em up,"   "THREE FOUR!"
"Kick 'em around,"

      "ONE TWO THREE FOUR, THREE FOUR!"

Scowling magnificently, his craggy face guaranteeing mayhem, Divino stormed up and down the outside file. "Dress it up. Sound off like you own a pair. Castellani, get in step. CHANGE STEP, YOU DUMB WOP. Green, you're bouncin' . . . still bouncin', Green. . . . GREEN, STOP YOUR BOUNCIN'!" "Can't help it, sarge, damn boots too tight," the tall boy replied, from the security of an inner marching column. Divino's breath poured onto him from across the man's face on the outer file. "No talkin' in ranks, you dumb bunny, just hold down the motherin' bouncin'," and he guffawed suddenly, no invitation to continued infraction but a measure of forgiveness, malice, good will, and cakewalked in step back to the center of the moving platoon. He was a thick and powerful man, a little under six feet tall, a missing left ring finger all that stood between him and a kind of physical perfection. He was also a skilled, butter-jointed clown.

"Lemme hear it, you bunch of Wacs.

"O Brown had a pocket of cash,"	"YOU'RE RIGHT!"
"O Brown had a pocket of cash,"	"YOU'RE RIGHT!"
"Pick it up,"	"ONE TWO!"
"Pi-ick it up,"	"THREE FOUR!"
"Kick it around,"	

"ONE TWO THREE FOUR, THREE FOUR!"

Up front a few in the know strained for a look at Cherry, marching his group twenty yards ahead, but he gave no sign that he understood, or cared. Divino never looked. He had them bawl the verses all the way back to the company area, riding over the more conventional cadence-counting of the three other platoons, and silenced them as they swung into position behind the orderly room.

The company marked time until the three stragglers, the fifth platoon, limped in and into their respective parent groups, and Sergeant Braun appeared on the steps. He halted them, and gave them "At ease," regarded his realm for a moment, and smiled.

"Gentlemen. It's a real pleasure to see your bright shining faces. This morning, administrative duties on behalf of our absent first sergeant, laid up in the hospital, kept me from joining you in the field, where a field first sergeant is paid to be; they will also do so this afternoon. Yet you all know that in spirit I am out there with you, keeping an eye on each individual uncooperative ass. Behave accordingly. When you get out on that obstacle course this afternoon, do your finest work, because rumors exist to the effect that the battalion commander will be in the area. If he is not pleased with what he sees, he hops on the captain, who has no choice but to hop on me. This is what we know as the chain of command. In my turn I am forced to hop on the platoon sergeants, who then give the business to their platoons. So who gets it in the end? That's correct. You ream yourselves when you put out less than your best. This is the thought I would like to leave you with. Now I disremember which platoon is supposed to eat first Wednesday lunch, and I know I can't trust you people to remind me, so what we are going to do is stand at attention for a while, and the sharpest-looking platoon is going into that mess hall first, and so on down the line. Atennshut!"

A bristling, palpable silence gripped the field. Braun removed a clipper from his pocket and worked on his nails for a minute or so. Finally he looked up, and threw a quick glance at each platoon.

"You're all looking pretty good out there, you four platoons, with some individual exceptions, and I want you to look at least that good in this Saturday's parade. I would say from here that the embattled second platoon, under the guidance of Corporal Cherry, is our winner for today, followed by the first, fourth, and third. Second, first, fourth, and third. There is the order for the meal. At ease! I have a message here from the old man, which is to bring your smiling faces back around these steps at twenty to one, for a little talk on a subject dear to everyone's heart. Right after mail call. That is all I have for you. Atennshut! First platoon, fall out. . . ." With a flourish he cupped his hand behind his ear and cocked his head toward the second platoon. "Do I detect a voice or more raised in protest? A second platooner anxious to know why he winds up eating last, even though Sergeant Braun just told him he is eating first? The reason is that our friend George Washington Brown turned his ugly face for a sneak peek up here right after I got finished telling you how nice and soldierly you looked. While you were still supposed to be at attention. Now this goes by the name of idle curiosity. You all know you've got to have every man doing his best, because one bad apple spoils the bunch, as they say. Fourth platoon, fall out! Divino's platoon, the sloppiest as usual, you're eating third today through the grace of God, fall out! Second platoon, go!" and spun around, and walked back into the orderly room. The brief drama he set in motion below would not have surprised him.

"You son of a bitch," said Griever, a wide blond from Tennessee. "You cain't stand still fo' a minute, can you. You got to move yo' ugly face. We'll drum up a little somethin' fo' you to move around about after lights out tonight."

"Man," Carver whined, "I never *moved*. That Sahgt Braun, he lyin' to you." His face worked violently under the impact of thought. "That chow the same five ten minutes later anyhow. What difference *who* eat first?" He was jostled by two more of the men he lived with, walking toward the mess hall. They regarded him with hate, threatened vengeance. They passed.

"Shee-it," Carver mumbled. He dug a boot heel into the earth. "Tonight still a long way off. I ain't even goin' to worry 'bout it."

When Captain Palmer appeared on the orderly-room steps promptly at twelve-forty to give an extemporaneous talk on social disease, he found he had a live audience, delighted to have put an unscheduled meal of C-rations behind it, bound by a collective grumbling as well as anticipation for the holiday, susceptible to and even eager for commu-

nications from above. He was a lean twenty-six-year-old
Virginian with sharp, delicate features and sun-colored hair,
concealed now beneath the white helmet liner, set low
over his eyes. He was a college-trained ROTC officer, but
his origins were buried under three long years of military
abrasion and blood: he owned an excellent war record, and
he was no stranger to command. This would be the third
company he had run through since being sent to Georgia,
and, while a basic-training unit brought its unique problems,
required a shift in the delicate balance between cajoling and
force with which one handled a combat outfit, he had succeeded in mastering these new techniques to his own satisfaction.

"Do you men *like* basic training?" he began, in the thin,
reedy voice he had trained to carry, and good-naturedly
imputed the proper meaning to the good-natured, garbled,
answering roar. "Is this the best damn outfit in the best damn
camp in the United States?" The catechismic roar. "With
the best damn cadre?" The roar. "And the best damn mess
hall?" The roar changed in character, increased in volume,
and Palmer raised his hands. "Any of you men want turkey
tomorrow? And cranberry sauce? If you do, you've got to
give Sergeant Mentor and his cooks a little breathing space.
C-rations today only mean that you chow down that much
better tomorrow. Does that make sense?" The crowd replied. "Let me hear you now—anybody out there who *likes*
turkey and cranberry sauce?" The wild animal roar.

To the rear of the crowd, almost detached from it, Roger
Hines, laden with contempt, watched the mad mob display.
He wished fervently that Palmer would get to the point,
deliver whatever idiotic message he had summoned the company to hear, so that Hines could move off into the shade
of the barracks and rest for the minutes remaining to the

noon hour. He would not be able (even after Palmer dismissed them) to drag his perspiring, weary body into the barracks and plump down on his bed, as he longed to do. The barracks were off limits during the noon hour. The urge to inspect might grip the captain at any time during the course of an afternoon (went the rationale), and a barrack had always to retain its buffed, dusted symmetry. Of course (Hines thought bitterly) violations resulting from the full-scale invasion which took place shortly before the men marched out (if the heat held) to permit the replacing of field jackets—the heel marks, the dirt, the beds nudged out of line—were easily distinguished by a U.S. Army captain from other, illicit untidiness; naturally (thought Hines) Palmer could identify outrages perpetrated during the legal assault and weighed, in his evaluation, only the dirt remaining . . . but he derived only minimum comfort from his irony. Pure malice, nothing else, accounted for the thousand stupid, niggling rules that contrived to make his life a misery. It staggered him to think of the brain power devoted to being asinine.

He watched Palmer's thin lips move soundlessly in the distance, and he wiped his forehead with his sleeve. It was hot . . . as brutally hot now as it had been cold in the pre-dawn morning, and he had known that it would be—but the knowledge was never enough. To be jolted from sleep by the sudden flood of light and the CQ's bark; to be compelled to abandon the cultivated warmth beneath the two blankets in the double set of underwear and face the unheated barracks: these were shocks it required his entire being to withstand. While others shed the extra socks and the longjohns and hopped about for warmth, while others dressed rapidly and trapped what heat remained in their bodies, Hines, numb with cold, stepped stiff and dreamy

into his fatigues, still clad in the winter (over summer) underwear, unable to deal efficiently, in the clasp of the frigid
Georgia morning, with the fact of the sweaty Georgia
noon, although he conceived of it; he simply was not able
to calculate the suffering.

While his mind wandered thus within the soundproofed
halls of his unhappiness, the captain's speech unfolded, and
was well attended. The subject of gonorrhea, and of the five
fresh cases reported in the company, was not without interest, and almost everyone paid close attention to the com-
manding officer's exhortations. He made it plain that he
was not happy with the fresh outbreak, not so much because
it tarnished the company's record—which was worth taking into consideration—but because of the downright un-
wholesomeness of this disease. He did not believe it necessary, as he put it, to "get the clap in order to have a good
time." There were pro-kits available in the orderly room,
there was a clean, decent club or two in town, but best of
all, for recreation, there was the post beer hall. He could
restrict them all to the post until the end of the eight weeks,
starting with the holiday tomorrow, but he did not like to
do that. He preferred to trust them. He had found that
(once warned) his boys could be trusted. Besides, not only
did they risk incurring his displeasure through disobedi-
ence, but ". . . Dorothy wouldn't like it. She wouldn't like
it a little bit if I had to tell her that some more of my boys
have gone into town and come back all fouled up, no good
to the company, no good to themselves. She's a pretty sensitive gal, and she's upset by information like that. So think
of Dorothy, and think of me, those of you who go into
town. Have fun, but keep yourselves clean, and keep the
record of Charlie Company the same way. Are there any
questions?"

It was Frazier (for not many else would dare) who popped his large calloused hand into the air and queried, in the broad accents and at the top of his voice, "Now just who in the name of Christ is Daaaathey, suh?" and earned the captain's hard, bright-eyed stare; but the acne-ravaged face was the face of someone wanting desperately to know.

"Dorothy happens to be my wife, soldier. I thought I had mentioned that before. Are there any other questions?" But there were none. Sergeant Braun called the company to attention, and released them, to idle away what remained of the noon hour. The captain returned inside.

"His wife," Frazier said meditatively, for the immediate few. The accent was nowhere apparent now. "I thought he meant the Dorothy I knew, that little old clapped-up Atlanta whore," and moved off purposefully, knifing through the slowly dispersing crowd, in the wake of Roger Hines, who moved crablike toward sanctuary.

Hines limped around to the side of the barracks and lowered himself in its shadow. He slipped out of his field jacket, laid it across his knees, and dug his shoulder blades into the wall. He shut his eyes. At once he opened them, sensing the intruder, and his stomach dipped in fear and anger as Frazier dropped to his knees and swung into position beside him.

"Doesn't he make your belly crawl?" Frazier said. "That patronizing so-and-so. 'Dorothy wouldn't like it. *Daaathy* wouldn't like it.' Who gives a shit what Dorothy likes? Of all the ways to appeal to a group of men to avoid the clap, that has to be the guaranteed worst. Dorothy! That paternal son of a bitch. Not only do we have Marse lookin' after us poor old disease-prone field hands, but Missy, too. . . . Did you know that Palmer was from Virginia?"

"I had no idea," Roger said loudly.

"A son of the Southland," Frazier said, and produced a slow, confidential smile. "Like me. And Griever. With certain differences. . . . Who do you reckon has contracted the dread disease?"

"I have no idea," Roger said, and watched an image of himself rise lightly to its feet, stretch casually, and stride off, sweat-free and unconcerned, into the sunlight; himself did not move.

"No idea," Frazier echoed. "I don't either but I can guess pretty well where they got it. The Mayfair. Julian's. The Star. You been to town yet, Hines?"

"No."

Frazier produced a pack of cigarettes and offered one to Hines, who shook his head. Frazier lit his own. They sat side by side, their backs pressed against the boards. Frazier's face was turned toward Hines, who stared out in front of him, at some point in the grass, his glasses dangling from his hand. The flat tan profile did look reptilian, Frazier thought, but helpless (less a copperhead than a garter snake, or a frog), and he felt a faint twinge of disgust, but he did not turn away. "You're not missing much. A desiccated, soldier-hating hick town is all it is. I've been in only once myself. I usually get a lift into Atlanta over a week end. There's a nice little town. It's a hundred-fifty-mile drive, but it's worth the trouble. Takes your mind off this military horse-shit for a while. Have you . . ."

"I have never been to Atlanta either," Hines broke in. "I have never left the post. I don't intend to. Look, is there anything I can do for you? Is there something you want?"

"Is there anything you. . . ." Frazier craned forward, and tried, without success, to meet Hines' eyes. "No, mister. There's nothing I can think of you can do for me. Nor is there a goddamn thing I want." He paused. "You know, you are about as unfriendly a cuss as I have ever met. You talk like a damn adding machine."

Still staring at nothing, Hines fell forward onto his knees, brought his uninjured leg forward, and prepared to rise.

Frazier's hand shot out and gripped his arm.

"No, look, Hines, I'm sorry I said that. It's the damn heat, makes a dumb rebel like me forget his manners. Maybe it affects you the same way. Why don't you just sit tight, and let's talk a while."

With a dull, pained look, Hines brought his eyes to the hammy hand that clutched his biceps, the thumb and forefinger not quite meeting around the bunched green cloth of his sleeve. Frazier looked at it too. Slowly, elaborately, he removed his hand, but did not otherwise move. Hines remained on his knees, poised; his eyes were still glued to that spot on his upper arm. *It takes as much energy right now to stay as to go,* he thought; but he did not move. The apology hung new and sticky between them, as if to have insulted him and then recanted gave Frazier a hold he could have achieved no other way. He felt he had to remain now, although he dreaded the encounter not less—more. He replaced his glasses and propelled himself awkwardly backwards. His helmet liner clunked on the tops of his frames, and his back banged into the wall.

"I noticed you noticing the ring," Frazier said. He flashed the fingers of the offending hand, and for the first time Hines saw the school ring. *I noticed no ring,* he thought, but held his peace.

"Jefferson College. Best four years of my life. You know, they pulled me off KP here one afternoon to do some typing in the orderly room, and I got a look at the company records. A pre-signal group is supposed to be hand-picked for brains over brawn, but I counted five college graduates

in the whole damn company. Three besides you and me.
That's probably why I'm always busy sniffin' around for
somebody I can talk to. A whole company of crackers and
Brooklyn boys is pretty rough on a snob like me. So I
come messin' with you every once in a while, though it's
pretty obvious you like your privacy."

Hines remained silent.

"The Army's not much of a place for privacy," Frazier
went on. "Or any of the other comforts. My idea is that
while I'm hooked I'll give it all I've got for the two lousy
years, but I feel only pity for the poor bastards that join
up, whatever their reasons. Things can never be that bad.
Take that Brown. I got a look at his record, too. He's an
eighteen-year-old enlistee, lives about fifty miles from here.
He probably joined so he could get the hell out of Georgia.
Naturally he winds up down here, being shit all over, and
with his kind of luck he'll pull a permanent assignment in the
South. He's a rare bird, though. I figure it would be the
same for him anywhere. What do you make of him?"

"What?"

"That Brown. What do you make of him?"

Hines made a quick-jerking movement with his shoulders,
and continued to stare straight ahead. Frazier was seriously
annoyed, but he masked it; he would have to force it a little
now.

"I've got a theory about that boy. Not a theory, just a
couple of ideas. I maintain he's got a special quality, something that begs to be kicked around, if you know what I
mean, and the capacity to seem to enjoy it, after it happens.
This makes him a pretty handy item to have around a basic-
training camp. On the one hand he makes it easy for the
cadre—he's a symbol of the company, and therefore a handy

whipping boy. They lay into him whenever anything goes wrong, or even when nothing does, just to keep the company on its toes. On the other hand, the men ride him because they've got to ride somebody, and here's this fella who is askin' for it. So he's not only our lightning rod, he's also our punching bag, gettin' it from both ends. It's like he went around wearin' a sign sayin' 'Kick me.' The point is, it's not a racial thing. I've noticed Negroes hop on him as often as anybody else. Northerners too, like Braun and Cherry. I'm inclined to believe it's got nothing to do with his color at all. Do you go along with that?"

Still Hines did not speak. *You're built for guilt, you black fool,* he had thought to himself that morning, trapped on the toilet seat by the man he had maligned by labeling him his worst enemy (for his worst enemy was the man he had until today so carefully, instinctively avoided, the man who pinioned and tormented him with such elaborate civility now). *You're built for guilt you black fool because you are foolish and black, and there is no deadlier combination,* and somewhere in here might lie a modicum of (intellectual) agreement with what Frazier had said, but he would never probe for it now. He shrugged a second time.

So Frazier marshaled his patience, and shifted his ground. His irritation was intense, but he was determined to elicit some response. To simply have Hines listening to him (once his goal) was no longer enough.

"Tell me, Hines, have you ever been South before?"

"No."

"Don't you have any curiosity about what it might be like in town?"

Hines turned to him for the first time. He met Frazier's blue, violent, impatient eyes, belying the mildness of his tone, and the sudden surge of anger melted to fear, and hardened again. *All right!* he thought. *If it's something he wants so bad.*

"I happen to be a Negro," Hines said loudly. "I have no curiosity about what it would be like to go into town."

Frazier smiled. "Well, now I know you're a Negro," he said. "Give me that much credit. I thought for that reason, as an *educated* Negro, you would want to go in and have a look around. In order to get the picture. I would take you in myself, if you could stand my company."

"What picture are you talking about?"

Frazier looked surprised. "What picture? The racial picture. Seeing firsthand what a man has to put up with in the South if he happens to be a black man. What you probably meet up with from time to time yourself. Don't tell me you haven't run into prejudice up North? Or in the Army?"

"Very little," Hines said. "Virtually none." He removed the liner, and drew his sleeve across the drops of sweat that stood out along the hairline. The long wool underwear itched unbearably. He looked at his watch, but it would not save him: ten minutes remained to the lunch hour. He decided to save himself. "I think I'm going to take a walk," Hines said.

"Wait!" Frazier said. "Let me just tell you something about myself. I see you're tense, and there's no need to be. Do you know what I was at college? Nothin' but a glad-handin', bird-brained fraternity boy, right into my senior year, and then one day the roof came down. I still couldn't tell you how or why it happened. There I was, boozin' and generally raisin' hell and not givin' a damn, and then there I was dropped from my fraternity for soundin' off against the bias clauses in the charter, damn near kicked out of school, losin' all my friends, and receivin' all kinds of strikin' notes in my mailbox. I just woke up knowin' one day, in spite of everythin' I'd ever been taught, that the Negro was as good as me, or would be, given half the chance, and if the sons of bitches I grew up with wanted to call me nigger-lover, well frig 'em, I learned to take it as a compliment. I took sides in a fracas or two . . . hell, I won't bore you with the details. I was drafted soon after, and here I am, talkin' to you. Rather, tryin' to. I can understand your reservations, but now you know. That all makes some difference, doesn't it?"

"Yes," said Hines.

"You're from New York, aren't you?"

"Yes."

"That makes you the first Northern Negro I've ever had the opportunity to talk to. Although I've been doin' most of the talkin'. I've been thinkin' of settlin' in New York, after my discharge. Sever connections with the Dark Ages, in a manner of speakin'. Maybe get some kind of job workin' with race relations. Tell me a little somethin' about the life up there."

There has to be some basis, some fact or facts from which he takes off, thought Hines. *He cannot have created, wholly from malice, such a sickly, elaborate lie.*

"I see you're interested in the Negro Problem," Hines said.

"Why, hell, yes. Haven't I just been . . ."

"I don't happen to share your interest."

"What?"

"I said I don't happen to share your interest. I have no desire to listen to your theories on Brown, or on anything else. No doubt it's rare and admirable for you to take such an interest. It's also excellent that you feel the need to broaden your horizons, and get the Northern Negro's point of view. Well, I must tell you you've chosen badly. I went to school with a brilliant boy from Chicago, a Phi Beta Kappa as black as the night, with racial consciousness and theories up to here, one of which was that you were obliged to reclaim individual white Southerners where you found them, and that's the man you want a conversation with. But so far fate has been kind. I have no intention of going into town and be treated as something different from a human being, although I suspect you might enjoy seeing that. I have no desire to be considered representative of a so-called ethnic group I feel no allegiance for. I have no stomach for being patronized, as you're patronizing me now. You've made a mistake. Whatever it is you want, you'd do better to look someplace else."

Frazier knew that this was not the case. He had what he wanted right here.

"If every Negro was as sensitive as you are," he said reasonably, "y'all might just as well clear some timberland and run up a flag. I'm not Uncle-Tommin' you, Hines, although you seem to have got that impression. I'm talkin' to you man to man. You can't help bein' what you are, you know that, but there's no need bein' ashamed of it, either. That's what the damn fight's about. Equal opportunity for all, regardless. When you say you're not interested in the Negro Problem, well now that's a lot of shit. You people have got to quit runnin' to extremes; bein' so damn conscious of your color that you think of nothin' else, or tryin' to pretend there's no difference between black and white at all. The point is the difference is there all right, but it shouldn't matter. Shit, Hines, I didn't mean to hurt your feelings, and I sure as hell wasn't Uncle-Tommin' you as you seem to think. I was only interested in gettin' your slant on things."

"You have it," Roger said. He struggled to his feet and

stared down at Frazier. "You have my slant. I want to be left alone. If there is one thing that interests me less than the Negro Problem, it's you. My only concern is how to cope with the Army. I don't need your help and I don't want your interest. So for the few weeks that are left, please find someone else to chase around and interview, and leave me alone."

While his usual pre-cut, strident delivery marked this speech, and his expression hardly changed, Hines' frail body trembled; for a second Frazier thought the boy might attack him, and he had to fight a smile. He could murder him, break him like a black, withered branch—and he would. But Hines made no such move. Frazier tipped the liner back onto his head and said, "Take care of your leg now, you wouldn't want it to get any worse than it already is," and Hines turned suddenly, wrenched himself around and started for the front of the barracks, limping more heavily than he needed to; for Frazier's benefit? he wondered bitterly; his own? loathing them both as he stepped out into the bright, merciless sunlight.

Around the corner from this painful private conversation Divino frolicked before an eager, sizable audience, his own men mostly, with a few interested additions from other platoons. He clowned with a limber marionette fierceness, a puppet gone loose and unstrung with humor and jerked now by its own residual showmanship, spinning and buckling and roaring and miming through the complex comic routines it seemed he would have needed to rehearse for, recruiting from the ranks indiscriminately as he required them the "volunteers," the sometimes willing and the more often wary (but the only risk that any ran was ridicule). On week ends he had his favorites (packing the Ford full with

them Saturday noon and sparing them the inconvenience
of the bus ride into town—forgoing the dollar a head other
car-owning cadre charged, but screening applicants with a
lot more care), but never in the field, and so in the field
during a break, or during lunch hour, he could admit to his
bias (rather glory in it) and lose nothing, but gain (if he had
made this calculation) in stature and appeal. This was one
of the few comic devices he repeated during the course of
any cycle, the one he repeated now, cutting short a highly
successful imitation of Sergeant Braun to lean suddenly
backward and propel his maimed left hand into the air and
rotate it lethargically counter-clockwise in a limp-wristed
parody of the military "Assemble!" but there was no mock-
ery in his face or tone:

"All Wops assemble on me! Assemble! Assemble! All
Wops assemble!" in the voice of command they knew could
dissolve at once into lisp or laugh or lady-like plea, as he
charged up the barracks steps and waited at a height to be
obeyed. Five men pushed to the front of the crowd to join
the three already there. All of them had, at one time or another, been chauffeured by him into town, and six of them
were members of his platoon.

"Now, you Wops," he began. ". . . We all Wops here?"

About half of the fifty men chorused, jocular yeas and
nays.

"All right. I want to know if you hear that dripping?
That's my ass bleeding for you. This here is no place for
Wops, especially if they have a little character. A Wop with
character should be doing midnight pushups around the
clock and collecting his twenty-six-a-week job insurance
and not be out here soldiering. The Army was made for
men, not Wops. But I want you all to get something straight.
We all Wops here? I want you to know that a Wop gets a

fair shake in Divino's platoon. Not that a Wop won't soldier, and not that a Wop won't sweat, but he gets taken care
of. On the other hand, every ass which is not a Wop ass is in
a sling. I'm going to jump it and I'm going to stomp it. It
gets no favors and it probably gets persecuted. This is the
message. Any questions? Any of you dumb Wop bunnies
got any questions?"

Somebody did. Somebody spotted a shuffling, muttering
Brown (freshly risen from the grass where Griever had
sprawled him) moving aimlessly toward the bleachers, about
thirty yards out from Divino's group, and somebody said,
"Ask Brown, is he a Wop?" with an oily anticipation and
Divino, unpredictable, complied. He brought his hands to
his mouth and he megaphoned "BROWN!"

The boy twisted to the sound his black mask of fear and
(when he saw from whom it came) indignation. He would
not allow Divino to join (at this late date) the ranks of his
persecutors, the one cadreman who had not, in six weeks,
taken advantage of (or created) the opportunity to molest
him. "Come on now, damn you mother, you messed your
chance up long before," he whispered righteously. "It too
late in the day for you to start to pick on me now." With
sudden hopelessness; despairing of his internal logic the moment he had worked it out, as he had been forced that
morning to waive the hope of marshaling an external one,
to squeeze in the latrine from the boy he thought he could
talk to (for Copperhead was not only bright, he was a
Negro, too) only a worthless, a lying reply. Man, he *didn't*
like to be always picked on (like Copperhead said), this was
no help, this was nothing but a lie. Yet here he was about
to be tripped up again (and from a brand-new source)
minutes after lifting himself from the floor. All he wanted
was to walk out to the bleachers to sit still until Braun's

whistle blew, to be left by himself, and he didn't move or
speak for fully five seconds after the sergeant's sharp command: "Brown, come double-timin' up here."

"If you don't mind, Sahgt Divina, I got myself enough
trouble right now."

"GET YOUR MISERABLE TAIL ON UP HERE!"

So then at a shuffling trot, mouth working, face lowered,
Brown moved up to and through the crowd which opened
for him until he stood at the bottom step at a form of attention and Divino, hands on cartridge belt and legs spread
wide, looked at him from above.

Divino's wild laugh burst into the new silence, and as
suddenly was gone. Then the sergeant was not standing but
sitting on the top step, leaning toward Brown, speaking
conversationally so that the back rows had to crowd in and
strain to hear.

"Carver, we got a little problem here that requires your
expert help. You a Wop?"

"What you mean?"

"I mean are you a Wop," Divino said softly. "Like me and
most of these other gentlemen here. Are you a Wop is what
I mean."

"Sahgt, I don't know," Carver whined. "I ain't never
thought none about it."

"Well you start thinking now," Divino said gently.

"Theah ain't no nigger Wops," Griever said scornfully.
He had ambled over to join the fun, and pushed up front,
when Divino hailed Brown.

The sergeant stared for some seconds at the newcomer;
then rose wearily from the top stair, removed his helmet
liner, and placed it over his heart. His exaggerated, imperfect accent did more for the calculated effect than a flaw-
less one could have. "Now, Tennessee, suppose yo keep yo

cotton-pickin' opinions locked up inside yo cotton-pickin'
face. Unless yo want yo dumb rebel ass down here on the
floor givin' me twenty-five. WHY, GODDAMMIT, MAN,
YOU ALL AIN'T EVEN IN MY PLATOON!" He
leveled his left index finger at Griever in this devastating
revelation. Then he seemed to forget Griever, and stared
at his fist. He opened it slowly and held it out before his
face, the hand so carefully concealed for almost six weeks
that only three of the trainees ever knew, spread his fingers
wide, and raised them over his head. With his right hand
he replaced the helmet liner, and then rested the hand on
the shoulder of Brown.

"Gentlemen, have you got any idea where Sergeant
Divino's ring finger is? Anybody got any ideas?" If any man
did, he held his peace. "I see I got to tell you. I left it in
Korea, fighting the common enemy, where all the jackoffs
go. Sergeant Braun has already notified you jackoffs where
you go if you don't shape up. You go to Korea to fight the
common enemy and protect democracy, like I say. I been
there. I froze my ass in winter and I broiled it in summer and
I got out in one piece and I killed my share of gooks, but I
left the live ones a souvenir. So hear this. The next jackoff
who pops off about who is a Wop and who ain't, which jackoff ain't even in my platoon, is going to wish he was stationed right now in his underwear on the thirty-eighth parallel, because that's how hot I intend to make it for him. Is
that understood? Now Brown, one more time, are you a
Wop?"

He was prepared now, having sniffed in Divino's attitude
the possibility of reprieve, a situation different from the
blind alleys he was accustomed to (with Cherry and the
others) where the contact itself was as good as the persecution: he had researched, holding his body rigid as he

turned his head so as not to disturb Divino's hand on his shoulder, and he had inquired (with little hope), and had miraculously received a reply (while Divino enlarged on his missing digit) from the boy behind. So he thought he knew the issue now (a Wop was an "Eyetalian"), and he thought he had a chance.

"Sahgt," he said, "My folks was never Wops, but I b'lieve I might be a Wop at heart."

Divino swept off his orange liner and slammed it against the railing. Brown recoiled. "There ain't no Wops at heart except WOPS!" Divino roared. "You understand that, mother? Now I get the impression you don't even know what a Wop is because I just heard you askin' that goofball behind. I'm going to inform you what makes a Wop, and then you're going to make up your mind. Either you are one or you ain't. And if you ain't . . ." The threat dissolved into high, demoniac laughter, in which the crowd joined. Divino's audience had doubled since he summoned Brown. He did not ignore it. He talked to be heard by the back rows now, although right at Brown.

"Now listen good. You're walkin' down a motherin' street at two o'-motherin'-clock in the morning. It's dark as a coal miner's ass; you ain't never seen it this dark. You got no idea where you are, you can't get off this street, you don't know how you're gonna get home. It ain't quiet. All around you in the dark you hear strange noises, people whisperin' or yellin' in gook, except once in a while you can make out your name. Now are you scared, or ain't you?"

There was, he decided dolefully, no right reply. He was in as much trouble (contrary to his earlier impression) as if Cherry were doing the baiting, or Griever, or Braun. Maybe more. He couldn't understand Divino at all. It made as much sense as anything else to give a direct, honest reply.

"Man, you right I'm scared," he said. "I never liked it in the dark."

"Good!" Divino said. "Good you're scared. Now listen. All at once a door opens on that dark street, and there is a nice warm piece of light where there wasn't none before. And back in there your shiverin', shakin' tail beholds a clean double bed with the covers turned back and a long cool rye and ginger and a wide-screen television set. And into the ee-luminated doorway blockin' your vision pops a big fat momma. . . . You like a big fat momma, Brown?"

"Yes, sahgt," Brown said morosely. He wondered vaguely what color that big fat momma might be, and felt a sharp new twinge of fear.

But Divino said, "Good. You're doing fine. Well, now, Momma knows when you're about to come pussyfootin' down that dark street because you're so scared you give off a stink, and she's lookin' out for you anyway. And she looks at you and she gives you the finger and the big hip and she says, 'Gohge Wash'ton Cahver Brown, honey, you my man. You's my tub-thumpin', dickslingin' happiness man. Listen to me, sugah. You all have wandered smack into Crud Alley, out of which hardly a man leaves alive because that is the way things are run heah. Y'all got a very slim chance to ex-cape which all depends on how quick you decide to cut a chogy because th' impohtant thing is speed, but theah ain't no guarantees, even if you was to start leavin' ten minutes ago. Y'all in a peck o' trouble, honey, and I want you to stop in heah and try to fohget it for a while,' and she opens that housecoat, Brown, and damn if she is wearin' a motherin' thing in the way of ladies' underwear. You with me up to here, you dumb bunny?"

"I understand, sahgt," Brown said.

"All right. So you got a problem. Because just then a red

light flashes on down the road a piece, and it says 'This Way to the Exit' and it flashes off again. And it flashes on. Then it flashes off. Now that light wasn't there before, and maybe it will never be there again, and you know your chances of gettin' out are slim anyway because Fat Momma told you so. You're breathin' hard. You look at Fat Momma. She looks at you. You look at the sign. It blinks back at you. You're sweatin'. You're thinkin'. You got a big decision to make. All right, Brown, what's it gonna be?"

"How you mean, sahgt?"

"WHAT YOU MEAN HOW I MEAN? YOU DUMB BUNNY, YOU GONNA slip it to the lady between the clean sheets like she is askin' or you gonna tuck it between your chicken legs and haul ass for the exit sign?"

He was dumb, but he was not that dumb. This time he read the signs. He knew well what Divino wanted him to say, but he still did not know what would happen to him if he said it—whether Divino was on his side or was his enemy, like the rest. But if the sergeant was out to get him, he reasoned, he would get him no matter what; oddly, this line of thought soothed him. He would tell the sergeant what the sergeant so obviously wanted to hear.

"Sahgt Divina, I guess I'd just as soon knock off that piece," and recoiled again as Divino's hand shot toward him, but only to clap him on the shoulder just before Divino shouted at the crowd:

"Look at him! A true-blue Wop! A Wop's Wop. Right?" To the first few rows: "Graziano? Boccia? He's a Wop, ain't he? You a Wop, ain't you, Brown?"

"I guess so, Sahgt."

"You GUESS so? You GUESS so! Get down there and give me ten, you mother." And when Brown dropped to the ground and laboriously began the pushups Divino straddled him, and just then caught sight of Cherry, exiting from the mess hall. So he leaped back up the stairway and stood looking down at Brown.

"Don't get up!" Divino roared. "You done your ten like a girl scout, but don't get up till we count the small change. Castelli, what's that fell out of that man's pocket?" while Cherry limped easily toward the orderly room.

"Nothin', sarge."

"Pennies! Did you say pennies? Brown, you jackoff, troublemaking son of a bitch, did you bring pennies out here onto the training field for me to bend for with my war wounds?" Divino whooped like a man in battle or pain, changed it to a high staccato giggle while Carver trembled below him and Cherry stopped finally, turned his head, and winged the hate over the yards like a shaft of light coming from his eyes.

So Divino breathed it. He stopped the noisemaking, and the antics, and he breathed it, what he had elicited for the second, the fifth, or the thousandth time. It was all he wanted now or ever from the Cherrys, the knowledge he was limned in spades for them (Divino!); to know they knew that from the civilian crazy core of him he hated their souls. Needing no crisis, no confrontation, no mundane test of strength (because he knew they feared him, would always fear him, and needed one less); he needed only this periodic (and mutual) affirmation of their polarity: that on a barren bloody peninsula blasting gooks with no names he could muster no love for, or in a basic-training camp crapping on people he sweated and created for eight weeks, Divino was Divino, Cherry was Cherry, and being in the Army changed nothing important, did not shape the guts of a man.

So once again he had it on record, where he had to have

it, and he made no more noise. He spun the instant Cherry did, and he disappeared into the barracks, leaving Brown stretched face to the ground and the disappointed crowd to wait for Braun's whistle, and he stalked into the latrine and he urinated, neatly and accurately, for he knew the captain planned to inspect the barracks that afternoon.

They screw their own, he thought. The image of the clean, delicate, wiry Captain Palmer burned through him now, and himself on hands and knees beside two corporals, three sergeants, and two other SFCs, scrubbing amidst a sea of suds at a wooden barracks floor while Palmer hovered briefly and scolded and warned it would happen again, oh, yes, men, with all the stripes and ribbons and purple hearts they had between them it would happen again if in future a group was allowed to move on with dust on the rifle racks and an ink spot on the floor—scrubbing the barracks floor and choking on it, a far more damaging indignity than being shot at even (because that was what you were there for); *They screw their own*, he thought, and then he amended, *That's only statistics, they set out to screw* everybody *and their own are around longer;* this the link between the Palmers and the Cherrys and the Browns and his own general unsuitability. And suddenly after six crazy years he *knew* it, there in the latrine, that the battle was over; that it was not enough for him (and never was) for the Cherrys to know that he was there; that when Palmer called him down in a week's time for the token re-enlistment talk SFC Divino would say *Captain, I'm thirty years old, unskilled, I have nine fingers, and I'm bugging out back to my home town in Ohio to look for a job. Because I can deal with the Cherrys, and if not for the Cherrys maybe put up with the Palmers, but with the combination, no—there is no way to educate that pig except to kill him and there's no way to educate you, Captain, unless it's maybe to quit on you and make damn sure you know the reason why.*

"SCREW EVERYBODY!" he yelled suddenly, startling the barracks orderly who lay on his bed, in a half doze, near the door. "Get off that rack and pull it tight," Divino shouted at him. "You ain't no privileged character. Don't you know the old man is gonna inspect shit out of this place this afternoon?"

"You bet, Sarge," the boy said nervously, but to Divino's back and the slam of the door. From the orderly-room steps Braun's whistle tweeted shrilly, the platoons assembled, and here began the unorthodox, ill-fated conclusion to the Wednesday afternoon.

Q7 loomed tall and complex over all the low-slung, less ominous field, the whole brilliant in the afternoon sunlight under coats of fresh orange paint, uniformly applied. Signal Corps orange covered even the rapidly rotating logs (maintaining-one's-footing-on) set in Q7's foreshortened shadow, decorated the barrel-sized iron pipes through which the trainees would crawl, brightened all except the barbed wire strewn at random in the jump pit, and the hempen rope descending at a forty-five-degree angle from the top of Q7 and attached to an orange pole fifteen feet from the floor (this device providing the trainees with an option, having met the first half of Q7's challenge, on the means of returning to the ground). Repairs and refinements had accompanied the paint job, part of a major base-wide overhaul completed only that morning, and Captain Palmer's was the first unit called upon to cope with the course in all its refurbished glory.

Q7 naturally caused most trainee comment, a centrally located Brobdingnagian ladder, rungs five feet apart, gaudy

pinnacle lost in the black blinding sunlight; to some a bona-
fide obstacle, to others a challenge, a lark to the few. Frazier
mocked it; he was a monkey in high places. Hines, who had
been excused, limped belatedly onto the scene behind the two
other members of the fifth platoon, regarded it briefly, gave
thanks once more for his injured ankle, lowered himself in
the shade of an evergreen, and tried to think about time:
basic training would be over in two and a half weeks (he
only half believed it), he would be granted a leave, and he
would go on home.

The eight-man cadre dispersed itself strategically over the
width of the field, determined to maintain order and en-
force honesty, but a form of chaos reigned. There were too
many obstacles and there were too many men going
through. It was possible for the enterprising lazy, by com-
bining adroit footwork with a moment of faculty inatten-
tion, to move around and past an obstacle rather than over
or through it, to join the disorderly queue which had just
completed it, and move on to the next; or, in some cases, if
an obstacle appeared particularly congenial, to double back
on one's tracks and repeat it, for a good part of the training period. Thus it happened that Carver Brown, muttering
but sharp-eyed, outfoxed Divino, who was supposed to see
that anyone who came his way took a running leap across
the barbed-wire-strewn jump pit (Brown shuffled around
it), crawled four times at his leisure through the thirty-foot
pipes (and was apprehended the fifth time by the sergeant in
charge, who imagined—and was appropriately vexed—that
he had caught Brown trying to sneak through for a second
time), avoided scaling a fifteen-foot wall which had no handholds, and spent a considerable portion of his time coping
with his balance on the rapidly rotating logs. But when carried inevitably to the base of Q_7, he was too outraged to

scheme. He would not even concede that it was something he wished to avoid, this nightmare of height and risk and ridiculous unfunctional labor; he would not even honor it by subterfuge, and head down he charged past its base (ignoring even its underside where grouped briefly those who had most recently completed the descent), moving blindly, laterally, back toward the beginning, toward the sidelines, toward rest, toward at the very worst scraping his belly on the earthbound ragged insides of the orange pipes once more. And he would have made it too—would have seen confirmed (what he had just learned from Divino) that he could abandon fear and caution and still escape punishment, just as a thousand times in the past six weeks he had mobilized caution and fear in usually vain efforts to avoid it; that there was no sense in and no way of predicting anything in the mothering Army—because Cherry gazed skyward at the moment Carver fled, upward past the creeping climbing succession of figures, fighting the glare with hands over helmet liner and checking on Frazier's whoop of contempt and power as he straddled the topmost rung; looking up (Cherry) because the whoop could have meant that someone was in trouble up there, too. So it was not Cherry but Griever who shaped what was to come, one of many who saw and were amused by or else resented Brown's flight from what some of them feared and almost all were taxed by, it was Griever who yelled after him in the unmistakable accents of the land where both were born: "Brown, you buggin' out again? Trot yo' ass back here and up this thing!" And even that didn't stop him (because he knew it as the voice of Griever, who wielded a different kind of power), although it slowed him down, and Cherry caught him; Cherry sprung silently after him at a light-footed limp and spun him around. The corporal didn't speak. He balled the back of the boy's sweat-

drenched T-shirt in his fist and dragged and pushed him
toward the waiting, growing crowd.

It was a reflex, not a plea: "Copul Cherry, naw!" in Q7's
hot, odd-shaped shadow, touching distance from the bottom
rung. Familiar ruddy fear replaced his indignation, flush-
ing him clean, yet he did not really believe that he would
have to climb the monstrous thing. Only his body knew: it
quivered as never in the cool black mornings when the white
man's razor flashed before his eyes in a cruel burlesque he
was not even aware of, as it never did when he was faced by
the venom of Griever, or the torments of Braun, as it had
never reacted before. Elaborately Cherry released his hold
on the T-shirt and put Brown away from him like a slug,
a thing picked crawling from his flesh, his mask of unfeigned
disgust having its effect on the watchers, but completely
lost on Brown.

" 'Copul Cherry, naw!' " Cherry mimed fiercely. "Naw,
Copul, don't make my shiverin' shakin' bugout ream-my-
buddy yellow tail go climbin' up that big old ladder. Let
everybody else do it, not me. You are a cowardly, worthless, cheating son of a bitch, you *hear* me, Brown. You been
under my skin ever since this cycle began, you're not fitten
to be a soldier. If I have to take any more shit from you
I'm gonna puke all over the field. Now move out. Climb.
Hand over foot. Foot over hand. We'll all be down here
rootin' for you. Climb."

"When I'm up high my haid spins, Copul, I mean it now I
never was no good at gettin' up onto high places evah since
I was a baby I fell off a porch and opened my haid took
twelve stitches. Copul Cherry please I'll KP ever night for
you and straighten up my area. . . . Shit, man, I can't climb
that motherin' thing."

One man laughed. The rest were carried blankly, smoothly,

on the music of the whine. Q7 stood bare, the last man having chosen the rope-pole route and shimmied to the ground.
Behind Brown the crowd swelled, some men approaching
for their second turn.

"Climb," Cherry said.

"Copul, if you listen . . ."

"Climb," Cherry said. "I'm giving you a direct order. I've
stopped my playing around. You know what a direct order
is, you've learned that much. So you go ahead and climb."

"Copul, I'll never make it. . . ."

"CLIMB!" Cherry screamed. He sneered at Brown's recoil,
but abruptly altered his tone. "Concentrate on what you're
doin' at all times. Don't look up and don't look down. Keep
your eyes glued to the individual rung you are working on
and move. Now move out! Move out, you chicken bastard!
Move out!" And he was not even sure that Cherry had not
taken a step toward him; he was ten feet off the ground
reaching for the third orange block before he realized he
had begun the ascent and scrambled up still another before
his momentum went, and he looked below him at the upturned sun-drenched faces, and started back down.

"Don't come down!" Cherry shouted. "Go on up! You're
doin' fine. Climb, climb, climb, or I will cut your chicken
heart out," Cherry sing-songed, reaching into his pocket,
"I just sharpened it this morning." And Brown did climb,
clambered upward to his own shock and surprise, driven
now not by unchanneled fear but the image of Cherry's
razor, catching the sunlight (although he had never seriously
considered that the corporal would cut him before). He
climbed, using to good advantage the vertical center strut,
suddenly deliberate and almost cool, talking himself up a
rung and then a rung more, watching his hands (but not his
legs), hand, leg, hand, until finally above him was one orange

rung, and above that was space, and broad sunwashed sky. There was no longer anything to reach for; he had a moment of panic, shut his eyes tight, and it passed. "Man, this is the top," he said aloud. "You done come to the top. Don't look down, Brown," he sang to himself. "Start on down, Brown, down Brown, to the motherin' bottom," he sang, and from below came a rich gravel cry: "Atta boy, Wop," and it moved him, hands gripping the center strut which extended a yard past the topmost rung; he thought *that Sahgt Divina, he not such a bad old mother, he don't give George Washington hardly ever no trouble at all,* anxiety flicking at him suddenly as he saw the need for different techniques, a new approach, in the matter of coming down. *I got to kneel first,* it suddenly occurred to him and slowly he inched his hands along the top beam, leaving it reluctantly, with great care, for the center pole, began to bend his knees, the left one pressed firmly against the strut and then (*like a sonbitchin' ghost,* he thought, not wondering how Cherry, with only his hands, was able or needed to achieve the banshee megaphone effect when he had heard Divino's voice only seconds before sounding loud and clear): "Browwwwwn. Yoooo don't come dowwwwwn yet. Stay right there. Yooo climb oooover the top and you come dowwwwwn on the ooooother siiiide, the oooother siiide, Browwwwwn. Ooooover the top. No goddamn cheeeeting, you understand? Do it right now or your ass is miiine, you hear me Browwwwwn?"

Please, motherfucker, Brown said to himself, and brought his right knee down flush with his left, his hands above his head and off to the left clutching at the center bar, a tableau of anguish, or prayer.

The echoic quality had gone. "Brown, I'm coming up. I'm on the way up and I'm going to toss you over the top if you don't straighten up and do it by yourself. Get up off your knees. Don't look down. I'm climbin' up to get you. You feel it shakin'? You feel the pole shakin', Brown?"

He thought he felt the pole shaking. Sweat dribbled off his forehead and ran into his eyes. "Naw!" he yelled. "Don't you come up! I'm standin' up!" He felt giddy with shouting, although he knew with a strange certainty that he would not fall. *Just hold tight, man,* he said to himself. *You keep your arms wrapped round that center pole nothing gonna happen,* and he blinked the sweat out of his eyes, pulled himself slowly erect, and once again over Q7's summit he faced the blue, naked sky.

"Oooover the top," came the ghostly voice from below; wasn't it closer now? Wasn't Cherry on the way up to make sure that he obeyed? "I *tole* you not to come up," Carver blubbered, and out of the sickening fear of Cherry behind him, and the expanse above (but Cherry behind him) he distilled enough crazy courage to work his hands once more above his head, to bear down on the flat smooth surface of the topmost bar, to pull and kick himself onto the summit —and he crouched there, clutching the yard-long extension of the center pole, all handholds below him, straddling the rung as Frazier had (in triumph) only moments before. From below came scattered cheers and ripples of applause. He heard them, and he knew what they were for: they were plaudits for Cherry, who even now scrambled up the ladder, five yards from him, a yard away, a foot away, and he sought the corporal, suddenly rigid with fear—down a rung, then two, then three, then drawn irresistibly in relief and terror he plunged his vision into the upturned faces, the pink and green (speckled with orange) sea. Naw! He shut his eyes. Almost immediately he opened them again, peered out past the training field, past the road, over the tops of giant firs and onto another road, a half-mile distant, where a doll-sized unit marched in ragged formation, rifles aslant, complete with its own limping stragglers, its own fifth platoon. *Oh Lawd!* Carver said, *I didn't mean to be up this high*, and glued shut his eyes. He smacked his cheek into the grained wood, released his hold on the center strut, and gripped the surface with quivering forearms and thighs. He bruised the numb, fatty, uncomprehending flesh, ground the skin convulsively from the left side of his face, slavered, and suddenly relaxed, awaiting the conclusion of the dream.

Roger Hines did not move from his leafy shelter, the fir's concealing shade, but he craned forward and upward, caught his lower lip between his teeth, and amazed himself. *If he broke his foolish neck there would be much less unpleasantness then*, he thought, and rebuked himself at once, severely, and with a great deal of surprise. But it was easier then: *If he fell there would be lots less pressure then. Less stupidity, less viciousness; the two remaining weeks might see this place a country club*, and once again inflicted a reprimand, experienced a guiltless rush of surprise. *I shouldn't feel this way*, he thought, and stopped feeling any way; his eyes traveled the length of the ladder, from the pressing eager crowd upward to the motionless clutching Carver (the highest part of him his green protruding rump, a study in fear) and focused there.

"That boy is crucified up there," Frazier said aloud. "He is paying for the sins of Charlie Company." He looked around—was it possible that someone within earshot might be worthy of the conceit?—but no one had heard. What had happened to that stinking Hines, who would barely admit he was alive? Was he taking all this in? It was he (with his bogus injury and phony detachment) who should be cringing and moaning at the top of the tower. Frazier searched the upturned faces of the crowd while Cherry bellowed through his paws, "Come on dowwwn, Browwwwn, all your friends waitin' on you down here," and Frazier gave it up finally and stared instead at the immobile animal sixty feet above the ground.

Divino performed a little jig, standing on the underside of the ladder, directly opposite Cherry, his hand gripping the bottom rung. He too stared into the sky. "You'd better go fetch him, Corporal," Divino said. "It appears his belly is glued," and laughed a wild man's laugh which could have fooled no man who saw his eyes. Cherry ignored him. He backed off and shouted again, louder than before, and succeeded in disrupting Carver's dream.

"COME ON DOWN, YOU CHICKEN BASTARD. I'M GIVING YOU THREE SECONDS TO START COMING DOWN."

"Lawd, shut up that noisy sonbitch," Carver mumbled, from lips pressed out of shape against the grain.

"Maybe he's a cat," Divino suggested. "He can haul ass up a tree when he has to, but he don't have no notion how to come down. Now you got to call the fire department." The few who heard joined tentatively in his maniacal laughter.

The color went from Cherry's face. His eyes never left Brown as he unbuttoned his fatigue shirt and shucked out of it, took off his helmet liner. With a cat's grace, and its speed, he ascended Q7, embraced the supine Carver at the summit with consummate gentleness, talked lovingly into his ear, pried loose his hold, enveloped him with his presence, and brought him, guided him, carried him down. The crowd held its breath, then cheered. On the ground again, disturbed, Carver sought to resume his jarred, garbled dream.

Cherry brought him to his feet. He would have slapped
him if he had to, but Brown's eyes were wide. The left side
of his face was scraped almost raw.

"You damn right you ain't gonna faint now," Cherry
said. "You son of a bitch you just committed a court-martial
offense, you know that?"

"I'm tired," Carver mumbled.

"You been messin' around and messin' around and makin'
this company look like hell right from the beginnin' and
lousin' up my platoon in particular, but you really stepped
into it just now, soldier, you disobeyed a direct order and
I'm gonna see it gets you ten years."

Brown wet his chin and rolled his eyes, from an older,
more potent fear.

"I'm puttin' it to you now. You're getting another chance
to go up this here ladder and come back down the right
way, under your own power. Not to be carried down by a
man with a game leg. Up, and down, and you're off my
shitlist, that fast. You don't have no choice, buddy, I'm
orderin' you up one more time."

"I can't sleep," Brown said.

"Whaaat? You can't do what? Why you lowlife bugout
yellow troublemaking ugly sneaky crawling son of a bitch.
You want to sleep? You want to sleep for the next twenty
years in the stockade? I'm warning you. Climb!"

Called him everything but a nigger, Frazier thought. *Even
in that particular moment of stress. I have been right about
it all the time.*

What are they doing to him now, Hines wondered. *He's
down off it. I can't see a thing.*

You got to kill them or quit on them, thought Divino.
But you cannot kill them and *quit on them. You cannot have
it both ways.*

Brown dreamed that Cherry shook him, and dragged him closer to the ladder, but he experienced no terror. Even when he began to climb he was not afraid, although he was surprised: you do any motherin' thing in a dream. Halfway up he misstepped and swayed forward through the bars, caught himself with a lazy drunken agility, twisted his body and (one at a time) his hands, and continued the ascent on the wrong, the other side. A few men cheered, with half a heart. Cherry fought for himself. "Now that was all right. You just saved yourself the trouble of crawlin' over the top. Hit the top and start comin' down," fighting the need to add "You hear me, Brown?" He lowered his head and this time caught Divino's beetling bright-eyed stare—raised his eyes in time to see Brown ignore instructions once again, and with a smooth, nonstop movement hoist himself onto Q7's top crossbar and once more straddle it, in reverse position this time, and lower his right cheek to the familiar comfort of the grain.

"He's gonna shave the other side now," Divino said. "He's shaping up. What a crazy Wop. Come on down, Wop," Divino called; but no one heard.

"All right," Cherry yelled. "Don't go to sleep up there one more time." He strove for volume only. "If I got to come up for you again . . ." His voice gave out on the threat, and he hawked away the soreness. He sucked in his breath and held it, for the boy had begun to move: he raised himself slowly to his knees and lifted his arms and thought calmly *if you reach for the pole Carver and hold tight nothin gonna happen, even in a motherin' dream*, extended his arms off to the left where (on his first ascent) the center strut had been, closed his fingers, wrists, forearms on air, came lazily, lopsided to a crouch, and toppled from the tower.

A few men yelled, "Look out!" but this was a warning, while he was still on the rise, groping for the pole, so that the descent was made in an eerie silence which he smashed himself on the four-foot orange hurdle that broke his back, caroming from here into the jump pit (the perils of which he had so recently avoided), slicing his contorted puffy face on the exposed barbed wire, and it was with the blood the noise began. Cherry did not contribute; was not among the first to race toward Brown's crumpled form; did just begin to move in that direction when he turned (realizing too late) to the hand gripping his shoulder and received two blows, a four-fingered fist at his temple and a whole one smashing with devastating effect into the base of his throat; while Frazier remained rooted for a moment, too: he stood on his toes and looked wildly around (while the object of his search was staggering from tree to tree on the perimeter, being sick on the move) and finally had to settle for an exasperated shout directed over the heads of the scampering heedless forms: *"Where is that antisocial Northern nigger? Is he still above it all now?"*

It has always seemed to me that people who hate me
must be suffering from some strange form of lunacy.
—SEI SHONAGON

All You
Faceless Voyagers

Methinks, quoth Sancho, a Man can't be in great Afflic-
tion when he can turn his Brain to the making of Verses.
—CERVANTES

THE WORLD may kill you. All around them things
were happening to the purpose. Camus was seventy-
two hours from the finish in a fast car and a week removed
from official interment in the *Times Literary Supplement*,
a generally favorable comparison with the author of
Howards End. In Cologne the same day an eighty-year-old
Jew was threatened with sainthood through the mails upside
down on the cross, and admitted to anxiety from behind
bolted doors to a sympathetic press. In California, a still-

young man having a resemblance to Manolete entered the
stretch after twelve years amidst law books, reporters, and
piped Guy Lombardo, awaiting painless death for certain
crimes against the social body, and much troubled the gov-
ernor, the State Department very briefly, and the overseas
press. The only thing to fear besides fear itself was the
lunatic and the fast car and the ostrich's substitute for
bravery. On a one-funneled boat built in 1910 called *Jorge
Segundo* the second-class cabin smelled intensely of socks,
which was irritating but the price the traveler paid for not
paying the price, because potentially they were first-class
people. Not that there lacked, all the same, legitimate cause
for complaint: on the trip out from Barcelona to Palma
second class had been a private two-berth cabin with a sink
with two taps and delicious seaborne intimacy with his un-
wed Swedish lady in a papal country, but between Ibiza
and Alicante second-class passage was separate, dismal com-
partments with similarly-sexed strangers. (All he asked from
La Compañía Transbaleárica was predictability, not the
best of everything.) The girl shared the filthy basin and
the fetid air with three women and a male child who slept
on the floor and cried from eleven until two, after which
the girl slept soundly until the *guardia* woke her at three.
After seeing her cabin he thought himself lucky, for the
smell of socks was one man's smell, leaving all that acreage
with two bunks unoccupied. The others, alas, would come:
a young MD and a fat, gallused older man who wished to
sleep. But for the moment he was alone and hopeful with
the one other who lay in his underwear facing the wall. He
shoved his crippled Olivetti (accidentally oxidized with
champagne in their hotel room in Palma de Majorca on
Christmas Eve) beneath the bed and placed his disintegrating
blue plastic zippered suitcase next to the brown one which

stood by the washstand, and sat on his lower berth to wait
for the girl. Across and above the man raised up and turned.
He was youngish and slight, with a ferret's face and bright
red hair and large brown liquid eyes of terrifying eagerness.

"*Anglais?*"

"*No . . . . norteamericano.*"

"*Bon. J'aime les américains.*"

"*Es Usted francés?*"

"No. I am citizen of the world."

Now he dropped to the floor in his stockinged feet and
leaned over and touched his arm.

"I speak English *y alemán.* I am citizen of the world. *Vous
êtes journaliste?*"

"No, tourist. *Soy turista.*"

"Ah. I too am tourist. I am citizen of the world."

Well that was a fine thing to be in the narrow straits of
our times, but he was the sort of person who did not like
to be touched. But the girl stuck her glorious Nordic head
past the curtain into the cabin, saving him from discomfort
or rudeness, he would never know. He excused himself from
the intense, fulsome friendliness with good reason, he
thought (the midnight sun of Ingalill), and they went above
and held hands around the crowded circumference of the
deck and poked into the deck passengers' room, which was
rows of wooden chairs facing a blank wall like a cinema in
which nothing ever played, and into the third-class sleeping
quarters, a dim stinking community cave over the groaning
engines which looked as bad as any of the troop or slave
ships he had ever read about or remembered. So they had
a compensating drink in the first-class bar, which he would
have sworn a moment before they could not afford. They
watched the suave newscaster on TV's only station cast the
news in a manner no head of state or first-class traveler

could object to—border skirmishes in unpronounceable places, distant, impossible tragedies. (But of the rush among university students in Barcelona, where this couple had met, on Fidel Castro beards, a pretty tame rebellion, no mention.) By the time they left the lounge the island of Ibiza was well behind, but they could see the lights, and in the clear, starry night she fancied she made out the lighthouse, and their hotel, and the clock on the church on the mountain. Happiness, regret for its loss, mingled and rose from her like a child's perfume, moving him to quick tears of love for her little girl's wonder and joy. The best lay ahead, the best was behind. Fatigue and the wind drove them below at last, from the best moment since the trip began, or since they met, from the kind of moment that in his ignorance he would have ceased to treasure if they came more often, and Alicante was a new world ahead in the dawn they might witness if they went to bed now. So at twenty past ten he slapped her rump in farewell outside the contiguous, segregated cabins.

His own room was dark. In the light from the corridor he gloomily spotted a valise on the bed above him and one more on the bed across, but their owners were no longer in the cabin. The citizen seemed safely lost beneath his blankets, asleep in the darkness, the curtain around his bed undrawn. With luck, he would drift into sleep himself before the newcomers returned. From his jacket he removed his passport and wallet and crammed them into the pockets of his trousers. He took off the jacket and folded it onto a shelf beside the bed. He felt beneath the bed and touched the typewriter, then slipped off his shoes and socks. He pulled the denim curtain around the narrow bed and stretched out above the blankets. Then he noticed the

breeze, and that the smell had gone. He peered out. The
cabin's porthole, above the citizen's bed, had been opened
halfway. The breeze was warm and gentle. He turned for
brief moments, luring sleep, teased it awhile, let it flow
through him and drag him down—but the keys began to
jingle and the talk began. The talk was in French, distinct
and loud. A bunk squealed and he looked out through a
chink in the curtains, barely moving his head, and saw the
redhead sit up and stare through the porthole; suddenly
throw the covers back and swing his legs over the side of
the bed. He was fully dressed. The citizen looked toward
him, toward his eyes, and he slitted his eyes. Slowly, slightly,
he turned his head, and when he opened his eyes again he
could see nothing but the inside of the *camarote*. He heard
the citizen sit noisily on the lower bunk and put on his shoes,
still talking, and move toward the door, and switch on the
lights, but he sensed more than saw the glare; for the denim
curtain held back the light.

—Pardon . . . I need light. . . . It flooded him, and for
reply, blocking out that eager sudden face, he flung his arm
across his eyes. *Bueno.* The curtain fell to, he heard splashing at the basin and the click of the lights and Good night,
and again the unspoilt darkness.

He lay still. He had to go to the toilet. He put on his
shoes and groped down the narrow passageway to the
cabinet. Returning, he saw a sailor stagger through the hall,
outside his cabin, outside Ingalill's cabin, out of control,
spewing vomit on the walls and floor, moving away from
the toilet, a sorry seasick sailor on the calmest of star-
studded nights. The sick man reached the end of the
corridor, and disappeared up the stairway. A further reason
to dive into sleep, before the smell wafted through the cloth

curtain which served instead of door into his cabin, and
he hurried into the cabin as if sleep waited in his bed, but
not for long.

But he was already too late. Sleep had flown. Five minutes later the fat man entered, stripped quietly in the dark,
removed his suitcase, and grunted into the bunk above. The
younger man arrived an instant later, and the fat man
switched on the light. The younger man thanked him. They
talked quietly. There seem to be no facilities for hanging
one's clothes, the younger man said, but that was the least
of it, the fat man said; this was positively the oldest and
worst ship the monopoly allowed on the line. The younger
man was not stopping in Alicante but was going on to
Madrid, and the fat man said that according to the papers
it had recently snowed in Madrid. The younger man (but
they were only voices now—he would not see the doctor to
know him in a professional or merely embodied capacity
until five in the morning, and the fat man at eight, waiting
to disembark, staring at him puffy and joyless like a shorn
Santa Claus, much behind in sleep), the doctor, crawled
into the lower berth across from his own, and the fat man
switched off the light, and curtains swished above and to
the right and he was alone once more in the dark with the
faceless travelers and his wholly triumphant wakefulness.
Really, though, it did not matter—he would try to sleep, he
would lie there until sleep came as it would have to come
before the dawn, and he would wind up sleeping two or
three hours, but it did not matter: the day ahead would
be warm and fine and they would find a hotel with a hot
shower and leave their bags behind and eat better than they
could afford to in the new city to hold off fatigue and then
they would go to the beach and he would sleep for a few
hours in the sun. In the corridor were sounds of gaiety, but

seven cabins faced off the passageway, and it was reasonable
to hope that the sounds would pass him by. It was reasonable because citizens of the world who jingle their keys and
talk to themselves and poke their heads into your bed while
you try to sleep are difficult to believe in after one exposure;
it was reasonable because if these acts really took place they
were perpetrated by a madman; and how many madmen
could be traveling (in his cabin) between Ibiza and the
mainland on the first day of the new year in the second
class? Yet when the sounds burst into the cabin, he was not
really surprised. Beyond his cocoon the light blazed again,
and silently, stealthily, he placed his arm on his forehead,
almost covering his eyes. He stared at the dark, wild voices
that issued from the space between the sink and the door,
and he pictured the cipher above, nonplused at the row
inches from his head, wondering whether to wait out the
tumult or take action and end it—for certainly, in the wide
Latin world, there must be people braver and more given to
active indignation than he. But from neither above nor across
came any sound to acknowledge or discourage the joyful
argument. High-school French brought him piecemeal to
the heart of the matter: the citizen had befriended and
rescued a stranger from third class or worse, and was
begging him to spend the night in the cabin. —There is
plenty of room, see, don't be an idiot. Things were moved,
suitcases were moved from the area between the sink and
the wall. —My pillow and both my blankets are yours. I
demand you stay. Try not to be a lunatic. The demurrers,
the grateful, less frantic but louder, drunker refusals were
laced with profuse, impersonal apologies. Excuse me, all of
you, pardon this mad, drunken, ill-considered debate between friends, forgive the senseless shouting that deprives
you of sleep, and all at once, *alors, bon,* a new wonderful

silence came to the cabin. The voices trailed down the hall.
From above now safely issued an imprecation, a fat man's
groan, a remark on the absence of luck and the healing
powers of sleep, a click, and the cabin became a crypt, hymn
to silent darkness. By comparison. The engine throbbed and
the light filtered in from the hall and (it sounded like) loose
metal balls rolled and clattered in the walls and it did not
matter anyway—sleep was a myth, and he had to go to
the toilet. He sat up and rubbed his eyes. His plastic suitcase
lay on the red-haired fellow's bed, a nice blue piece in its
time, its metal skeleton poking through its ruined sides, its
zipper cranky now, precariously placed atop the man's own.
The citizen's pillow and blankets were on the floor. Now
that was the limit, tampering with private property, and
he snatched up his suitcase and shoved it under his bed. Then
he slipped into his shoes and went to the toilet. He was
gone about two or three minutes. On his return someone
moved about the cabin. He saw poorly without his glasses,
which were tucked safely in his jacket pocket on the shelf
next to his bed, and he mumbled a greeting to the man
bound for Madrid, realizing his mistake even before the
narrow, eager face pushed into his, and the conspiratorial
hand gripped his arm: "*Écoute . . .*" Wordlessly, roughly,
he disengaged himself, pain and disgust clear on his face
in the flickering light, slipped quickly out of his shoes and
took possession of his bed. "*Pardon,*" the citizen said (what
had he done? stepped on the body below?), thudding into
the upper berth, dropping his suitcase to the floor. For some
seconds there was the silence of the engines and the silence
of the metal objects clacking in the walls. Then the noise
began, the earlier impossible sounds insanely magnified: the
keys he jangled were bells, the voice in which he spoke was

meant for thousands; now too he discovered a musicality, a pernicious, perfect whistling through Spanish love songs, and now too he opened, and gazed out, and slammed shut and reopened the porthole.

The fat man groaned, an equivocal sound which could have been made in his sleep. He could no more be asleep than the redhead himself. Hearing the guarded protest from above, he wondered if it were more or less hypocritical than his own paralyzed pondering on the possibility of changing cabins—which he would not act upon for fear of inciting the citizen and the difficulty in explaining matters to the people in charge if he had known where on this disorganized tub to find them—he decided no, the groan was not more hypocritical; he therefore fixed on an arbitrary, undefined breaking point (five thousand bilingual words? six or seven well-whistled airs? within these limits the citizen could tire; madmen sleep) reaching which he would spring from the bed and say listen here, you, it's time to write 30 to this antisocial crap, or he would say nothing but pick up his Olivetti and his bag and seek refuge through the reeking corridor in another cabin. So he lay still in his cradle while the old ship nosed toward the mainland, creasing the flannels and the drip-dry shirt, figuratively counting the words.

The citizen's remarks were in the main unkind. Ibizencos were a narrow, bitter people. Alicante was a joke of a town. Spain was in sad condition and a franco, a new franco, was worth twelve pesetas, no more. Twelve pesetas make a franc. *Franco vale doce pesetas.* His French was fluent, Spanish nearly so. His whistling was almost professional. What he saw when he looked from the porthole might have been beautiful. Most interesting of all to contemplate was the distress of the others, the cautious groaner, the Madrid-bound sufferer in silence. Forewarned is forearmed. They had had no notion they would spend the endless night with a screwloose citizen of the world.

But when the man fell silent, and remained silent, he was nothing if not grateful. He looked at his watch in the dimness and read twelve-fifteen. It was not as late as he thought. To sleep from one to seven, no more, would render unnecessary his elaborate phony compromise—hot bath, huge meal, nap in the sun—six hours' uninterrupted sleep was all he asked of God and bedlam and his body. Yawning silently he turned to the wall.

"*No bueno.*"

It was almost a whisper. The sounds of moving about, dropping to the floor, were strangely muffled, as if in consideration for people asleep. Even the light clicked on gently, and since he could not now see the light (his face to the wall) he refused to acknowledge any of it, the sounds or the light or the wild beating of his heart.

Above him the curtains screeched apart. —Sir, I would like to talk with you. . . .

—No, no, please, I want to sleep, the fat man cried. I have to sleep.

"*Ah. Pardon. Mil pardons.*"

The curtain clattered shut, and the tap ran. The water, on full blast, smashed into the basin. Slowly, soundlessly, he turned over onto his back. The water ran. Slowly, silently he brought his eye to the crack between the curtains at the instant the curtain dissolved and left him face to face with his tormentor.

"De Gaulle is excellent leader, do you not think, *journaliste?*"

"Yes. Yes."

"Listen to me carefully. . . . I have much information of de Gaulle."

"I am not interested. *No me interesa.* Why don't you go to bed and let other people do the same?" and again, with an arm, blocked his eyes. The curtain remained open. The piercing whistle rode over the splashing sounds. He opened his eyes. The citizen stood at the basin, combing his hair. The citizen stared into the mirror above the washstand and the bright, eager eyes met his own, he knew, although without his glasses he could not really see. The torrent ceased. The whistling stopped. The redhead brought his face up close to the mirror and gripped his hair.

"I speak English! Americans hypocrites! Filthy American *journaliste* hypocrites!" More came in a garbled German and rapid French he was content not to understand. He pulled the curtain to, but the halves did not meet, and he saw the citizen approach his bed and kneel by his bed, still talking. He did not move. There was a scraping sound, and his suitcase suddenly appeared in the middle of the floor of the cabin. The redhead straightened and shut the light.

"*Bon. Bon. Me voy. Adiós. Buenas noches.*" But he fumbled and poked some more in the dark in corners of the cabin. "*Adiós.*" In each hand he held a piece of luggage, this much was clear through the myopic fuzz as the man walked through the curtain into the corridor.

He groped for his glasses, could not find them, leaped from the bed, and stuck his head out the door. The citizen neared the stairway at the end of the corridor. He could not see what he held in his hands. His blue suitcase was there all right, he tripped over it when he went to squint down the hall, but the typewriter! He dropped to his knees and reached frantically under the bed, hand, arm, shoulder, and he touched it, shoved back against the wall by his own blue case when he rescued it from the stranger's bed and pushed it beneath his own. He looked around him in the dark, to share his relief. There were no signs of life in the other *camarotes*. He could not blame them. The man below had not been molested. The man above had been permitted to sleep. Two large suitcases stood by the washstand. It appeared the red-haired man had stolen nothing; picked up his own luggage and abandoned the cabin. Perhaps he had gone above to watch the stars. Perhaps he had gone into steerage to join his friend. What was the difference? The lunatic was gone, bag and baggage, into the unlikely world from which he came.

He was tired enough to sleep, but it took a little time. Footsteps outside, alerting him, turned out to be en route to the toilet. Stealthy noises were mostly in his mind. At last his body took charge, that fallible arbiter, and the next waking thing he remembered he would always remember.

He dreamt a grimmer, fitter ending to the small fraud in the harbor. As it had happened, they strolled slowly along the seafront, pausing to admire the scuttling sea things, invisible to most people, she had discovered in nooks and crannies in the palings of the wharves, halting longer to consider, not for the first time, the upright corpse of the cat, levitated midway in five feet of water in the corner of the harbor, astonishment in its wide, gleaming eyes, about to spring, continuing on in the balmy December morning past the sailboats and yachts and fishing smacks until they reached the wharf where the ancient, awkward rowboats were. She spotted a boy dozing in a sailboat at the end of the pier, no one else in sight, and they went over and woke him gently. The price was ten pesetas an hour. They rowed straight across the calm and clear blue stretch, shallow as a lagoon in some places, to the beach they had bicycled to the day before, then along the bank out past the lighthouse jetty to where the water darkened and rippled and roughened, becoming without transition the open sea. He bounced bravely into the black, choppy waves for a couple of yards before they both became frightened, turned with difficulty and worked the cumbersome boat back into the abrupt safety of the shallows. They shifted seats and she rowed them home. The boy was gone when they returned. Across the road was a fisherman's shack she wanted him to look into. Ten pesetas would buy four *coñacs* along the Vara del Rey, but he peered into the shack and found three old men playing cards. "*Buenos días . . .*" he began; they mumbled perfunctorily and looked away. Explanation was pointless. He shrugged, grabbed the girl's hand, and led her back toward the hotel, three times glancing stiffly over his shoulder. The cat eyed him balefully when they turned the corner. The girl hummed to herself. No one pursued.

This time the cat struck, and the furious, screaming boy closed the distance behind. As he turned to face him and pay him the girl disappeared, and the cat tore away his glasses, so he could not see the face clearly, even from three feet away. He could, however, see his hair, the flaming red of the citizen's, brilliant enough to alert the dreaming blind. From the dreamy funk came cracks of bone on bone, nothing he could hope to see any more or feel, either; the fists landed with blurred speed and painless shock out of the nightmare one wakes out of more often than into, but next he was seated in the dried vomit (at three a.m.) of the drunken Spanish sailor and scrambling backwards on his hands, away from the crimson center that pursued him on a treadmill, never more than a yard away; he stood again, moving backwards, and he dreamed for the first time in his

life in Spanish (to prolong this colossal conceit), he heard
himself referred to as the son of a whore, which was absurd,
and about the time of the next crunching blow in the face
he became aware of the butterscotch sound, the syrupy
moan of naked terror, which had begun before this moment
and would continue after it although he knew it was himself making it and though he would have liked to stop, and
he was down in the slime again scuttling backwards on hands
and bare heels and standing again, and here came speechify-
ing murder, talking steadily into the pleading howl, a yard
away as usual, and moaning, he struck a blow. It must have
been a glancing left, because later, on the knuckles of the
little and ring fingers of that hand were the brave half-moon
cuts which were all he would salvage from New Year's Day,
1960, except his property and his life. It felt pretty good to
hang one on Death, and with his own weapon too. But he
was down again, and this time he knew why: somebody
alert and alive had hit him in the face. Somebody had
smashed him on the ears and mouth and eyes with a mace
and blind and terrified or not he could see there was no
help forthcoming from the cabins off the corridor. The curtains were being pulled tighter around the *camarotes* from
here until the end of time.

"*Bien. Basta.* Good-by."

He saw the citizen turn, and go, but he moved backwards
on his heels and hands another six feet before he stood and
staggered to the stairway. Reprieved! He carried his noise
with him into the second-class dining room. It was less than
involuntary now, it was more than merely terror, it was
louder now, the deliberate prolongation of the fruits of
waking nightmare resolving into a cry for help: *Listen to
this inhuman sound you sacked-out people, help me, or
poorly protected as you are you'll get the same;* they were

women, prone on the floor and benches and tables of the
dining room, preferring this to sitting up all night in the
screenless cinema of the third class, but the steward they had
tipped for the privilege sat dozing at a table and he made for
the white jacket and held back the sound and gasped out
words: "*Hay un loco abajo, un hombre loco,*" and the steward said —All right, calm yourself, we'll go and see. But the
mayordomo appeared from his cabin, shaking off the caul of
sleep, a giant, already half dressed, who regarded him briefly
and started down the stairway—the steward behind on the
narrow stairs and he behind the steward. The corridor was
deserted, but he sensed activity behind the curtains now; a
curtain lifted just off the stairway and an old man emerged,
a second steward, superfluous people both in the usual
course of events on the *Jorge Segundo* in the second class
because there had been no dinner and there would be no
breakfast—but there they both stood in their dirty white
jackets, and there coming down the empty corridor toward
the foot of the stairs was the citizen of the world and he
carried a blue suitcase.

The *mayordomo* stopped his progress by standing at his
ease in the corridor. —This is your friend? he asked. He
nodded dumbly. —Where are you going? the *mayordomo*
said, and the citizen said —Above, man, above, and the *mayordomo said* —We will go with you. —No, the old steward
said to him, clutching his arm, you stay here with me. Suddenly there were people, a half-dozen jamming the corridor,
regarding with interest and horror the foreigner with the
battered face assaying calm in bare feet and vomit-stained
trousers and losing blood onto his chest from a hidden place
under his chin. O, the blood, a woman said. Until that moment he had not even seen it. He regarded it with disbelief,
for it came fast, dyeing the nylon as if generated by the cloth

itself, and he had no idea where it came from, and he felt no incommoding pain. But the old steward brought a stool into the corridor and gripped his shoulders and sat him down, and tipped his head back and mopped his throat with a wet towel. —The doctor is coming, the old steward said. I do this as a temporary measure.

"Are you English?" a sailor said. "I speak English."

"Do you have a cigarette?"

"No. I don't smoke."

Neither the steward nor the onlookers had any tobacco. "I will find a cigarette," the sailor said.

Slowly, the corridor cleared. One or two lingered, ultra-curious or insomniac. They sought information, but he was not helpful. The steward was bathing his wound. The sailor was looking for a cigarette. It was no longer urgent that the world, awake or sleeping, draw a moral from his accident.

"He has my suitcase."

"*Mande?*"

"*El loco tiene mi maleta,*" he said, *containing clothing which is replaceable and notes for a novel of uncertain value. The worst that will happen he will throw it overboard from some logic of his madness. I knew a man once had his Ph.D. thesis stolen on a train to Milan. I do not appear to be crippled.*

The steward did not understand. The sailor returned with an Ideal, 5¢ for a pack of eighteen. "The madman has my suitcase," he said slowly.

"Ah? I will report this to the *mayordomo,*" the sailor said. "I go upstairs at once."

He sat there (a carton of L&M in his valise) with the yellow cigarette that would not draw, the old steward hovering concerned and useless with the towel, promising the arrival of the ship's doctor imminently, which was taking a lot upon himself because the ship had no doctor, and after a while the *mayordomo* came hugely down the stairs carrying his suitcase.

"*Es la suya?*"

"*Si.*"

—You will kindly open it.

He tried, but someone, less kindly, had tried before; the zipper was torn, the clasp was jammed.

—If it is yours, you have the key.

—There is no key. I lost the key three years ago.

—There is no key?

—No.

—Then it may be opened easily.

—Someone has broken the clasp. Why must I open it?

—He says you have stolen his shoes.

The *mayordomo* looked at him shrewdly. He sat on a stool in the gangway dripping blood from his chin, his eye beginning to puff and darken, the blows already struck under and on both sides of the jaw which would make it seem for the next three weeks that his inner ears were tied to his cheeks so that chewing at all at first and then chewing with any degree of interest or speed would bring on a jerk of impossible pain much out of proportion to whatever he might have hoped for in the way of enjoyment. He was also barefoot. He could see, glancing at the *mayordomo*, that all this worked in his favor.

—I was asleep. I did not steal his shoes. He is a madman.

The *mayordomo* smiled. —There is probably some truth in that. He is upstairs now with the *guardia civil* discoursing on the stars.

—I can't get the case open.

—Let it go for now.

The citizen descended the stairway, jaunty, eyes eager

and fire-bright. He was smoking a cigarette. Behind him were two civil guards. The old steward hovered protectively. The English-speaking sailor looked interested. The young steward came down behind the *guardias*. As he moved by the stool the citizen made a pass under his chin with the cigarette, slowly and experimentally, as a child holds a match to a wingless fly. Now for many nights afterward he would lie stark awake in the Barcelona flat starting at sounds and perspiring and puzzling the mystery of sleep, for racking his memory he could not antedate his presence in the corridor, his helpless mortal presence in the corridor, as the true beginning; he could conjecture that the man struck the first, most damaging blow while he was in bed and he sprang up and out of the cabin automatically, in the interests of self-preservation, or he could hypothesize that the man shook him gently with the gentleness of the grave, said Come, come, and he went, but all he could re-create for certain was horror. (Someday, maybe, he would hire a hypnotist.) But at the moment he was no wingless fly, there was not all that difference between them, and he shot off the stool pulse pounding in his wound and was restrained by the stewards, the citizen already past him when he rose and wrong to move at all, he realized, given his station in life.

—What takes place now? the *mayordomo* said, smiling at the *guardia civil*, the one with the face of a horse, who replied,

—He has something of great importance to show us in the cabin.

—Well good, the *mayordomo* said, I will join you in a moment.

He heard the citizen's booming voice. He turned to the sailor.

"Could you do me a favor. . . ."

"What do you like?"

"My things are in my cabin. Could you bring them here? *Una chaqueta, zapatos, una máquina de escribir.*"

"At once."

The old steward, who had followed the *mayordomo* to the cabin, returned alone, his sunken mouth stretched wide.

—You should have seen it. The *mayordomo* delivered a blow. . . .

—You didn't stop the blood, he said. I would like to see the doctor.

—Still the blood! Do not worry. He will be here any moment. I will bring a fresh dressing. The steward disappeared into his cabin, to the left of the stairway, emerging with a freshly moistened towel.

He held the towel against the wound which would be cleaned and clipped together in Alicante later that morning by a government doctor with little ado. Six days later the stitches would be removed by a government doctor in Barcelona. Chewing would remain difficult, he would be summoned to the Maritime Office and questioned on the nature and extent of his injury, in order to determine, by some medieval magic, the length of the citizen's incarceration, and he would be advised by the American Consulate not to sue. That would end it. He accepted the steward's pottering attention out of politeness and because the towel might do something toward stanching the blood.

—The scream was monstrous, the old steward said.

The women, the sailor, and the two stewards remained in the corridor.

—It woke us all up, one of the women said.

—When I heard the scream I thought it was over, the old steward said. I did not even move from my bed. Once between Las Canarias and Cadiz there was a similar scream and a throat had been cut while its owner slept much in the same way as here. It is a terrible scream. Only one thought, the Italian word *finito*, ran through my mind.

—The bleeding has stopped, he said.

He was about to catch a last glimpse of the citizen. The procession moved down the corridor, but his back was to it. The steward faced it. The old man almost lifted him from the stool and pushed him into his own cabin. The old man quickly pulled the curtain, but not all the way. Down the hall they came, the *mayordomo*, the horsefaced *guardia civil*, the citizen, a second guard. The citizen was the citizen of a world the size of a pingpong ball, but his voice was unbroken, still unwinding. His nose was crushed bloody pulp, all over his face, and around his waist and throat were ropes of incongruous thickness, to drop an anchor by, which the second *guardia civil* held and manipulated, and stopped the citizen's forward progress at the foot of the stairway.

—Remove your trousers.

—The filthy Madrid fascists who misunderstand de Gaulle . . .

His head jerked backward.

—You will take off your trousers.

The redhead bent and with much effort, and briefly silent, removed his trousers. He worked them laboriously over his shoes, exposing white drawers and thin white legs, straightened and saw him peering from between the hastily drawn curtains. "Hypocrite!" he yelled, and began to curse, in Spanish and French, as the guard behind prodded him up the stairway. The old steward did all but bring the back of his hand to his mouth. He pulled the curtain completely shut and he said — Do not listen. Pay no head. Refuse to hear him. Do not remember, as the sounds died out up the stairway.

He parted the curtains. The young steward smiled at him.

—Who is he?

—A lunatic.

—Is he French or Spanish?

—He is too crazy to be Spanish. They think he is Algerian, but he threw his luggage into the sea with his identification inside. Nobody knows.

—He threw his own bags overboard?

—So it appears. Do you not think you should go back to bed?

—I'm not tired. Could you bring some *coñac?*

The young steward looked helplessly at the old steward, who shook his head. —The pantry is closed. It is impossible to get brandy now. Perhaps in the morning . . . If you had seen the blow the *mayordomo* inflicted. . . .

"*Fuck* the blow," he said. —Where is the doctor? My suit is ruined. My watch is destroyed.

—All will be taken care of when we dock, the young steward said. Don't upset yourself. The Company will take you at once to the hospital and clean your suit and pay for your watch. Now you should try to sleep.

—I'll sit upstairs awhile.

He put on his shoes and socks, he picked up his suitcase and his typewriter and jacket and went upstairs. On the floor and on benches and tables the classless people wrestled with sleep. He was fairly quiet. He fought the suitcase open on a vacant table and extracted a pack of cigarettes. The young steward came up and joined him. They puffed for a time in semi-darkness. There began the sharp, steady throbbing in his ear.

—You were asleep? the young steward said.

He nodded.

—He is definitely insane. You are very lucky. He used only his keys.

—Keys?

—He held them protruding between the fingers of his fist, as (the young man shook his head) he illustrated for the *mayordomo*.

He derived comfort from this information more useful still in weeks to come, flailing up from sleep with the yell on his lips beside the poor girl in the double bed, staring twice at redheads on crowded sunlit streets, heartsick peering through the aperture when the porter rang each day at noon to bring the mail. No wonder. Not merely shocked from sleep by a madman, but a madman armed; that keys were not lethal was the measure of his luck (throat not cut, loins not slashed); that they did greater damage than bare fists was demonstrated by the long jagged scar on his jaw.

—You speak Spanish?

He turned to the civil guard. —Some.

—It is necessary to ask some questions.

His nationality, his marital status, the date of his entry into Spain, his future plans, his occupation, his address, the nature of his quarrel with the citizen, the extent of their acquaintance, all came into question. He said that he had never seen the man before he entered the cabin; there had been no words between them; he had been asleep when the attack occurred; previously the man had kept all other occupants of the cabin awake by whistling and talking and switching on the light and playing with his keys. He mentioned also the citizen's dispute with his French friend. He did not mention the citizen's opinion of Americans nor did he dwell on his own refusal (a reasonable, sensible refusal:

a man preferred sleep to intercourse with the unwashed insane) to treat the citizen kindly. Yet that worried him now; he was at fault; you owed the nearest lunatic, on many counts, a measure of civility.

—You're traveling alone?

—My fiancée is with me.

—And where is she?

—Below, asleep.

—The girl is also North American?

—She is Swedish.

—It will be necessary to ask her some questions.

—She is asleep. She has nothing to do with this.

—Where does she sleep?

—In the cabin next to mine.

—Which bed?

—The upper, near the door. There is no need to wake her.

The guard disappeared below.

—Is there no coffee either? he asked the young steward.

—Not until six. What time is it now?

—My watch is broken.

—They do not open the pantry until six. I am very sorry.

He looked sorry. He looked sorrier at six, when there could be nothing until seven, and at seven, when the pantry would not be open until seven-thirty, and at seven-twenty-five he disappeared, as two dozen second-class passengers grumbled for coffee. He returned with three cups of coffee shortly before eight. One of these (since the others had begun to disembark) he drank himself, and the two remaining went to him and Ingalill.

—Why must he question my fiancée?

—He is the law. He questions everybody.

She came up the stairs finally, blinking, disheveled, saw him seated there in his spattered shirt with his battered face, and she began to cry. When he saw her last she effused a child's pure joy that enhanced her loveliness, and now she was a kid lorn and scared, no relation to the child before. Poor thing. An entire kindergarten, joyful and terrified.

He soothed her; he knew how bad he looked. He'd seen in a mirror in the old steward's cabin. The bumps swelled on his cheek and forehead, the eye had begun to close, the wound beneath the chin still bled, but he was recognizable, she'd get used to it. It hurt his ears to talk, so he gave it up, and stroked her hand.

"I wasn't asleep when he came in," she said. "He put on the light and looked in all the wrong beds first. He ordered me to dress and come outside. As soon as he came in the door I knew something terrible had happened to you. Those horrible yells. I knew they were you."

"Let's forget the yells."

"He asked a thousand questions, but he wouldn't say what was wrong. I thought you were dead. When I started up here I thought you were dead."

"He didn't have to wake you."

"It's better that he did."

"I feel so bad," she said after a while. "So rotten and empty."

"Try to sleep for an hour or two. There's no point your staying here."

"Your shirt . . . all that blood . . ."

He looked down at his shirt. "I'll change it." He opened the suitcase and took out a red, short-sleeved sport shirt, a gift earlier in the year from his younger sister on his twenty-seventh birthday. It was much too loud, and he wore it only at the beach. "I'll put this on."

"Why did he hit you?"

"I told you, no reason. He's out of his mind."

The *mayordomo* came up the stairs and paused at the entrance to his cabin.

—When it commenced, you were asleep?

—Yes.

—A rough awakening. He smiled. —But you now may sleep in earnest. Your friend is secure in another part of the ship. He's unlikely to bother you.

"You broke his nose, you fat prick."

"*Buenas noches,*" said the *mayordomo.*

"*Buenas noches,*" said the young steward.

She sat with him a while, querulous and numb. Finally he got her to leave. The young steward slept again with his head on his arms and the women slept on the floor and benches and he was alone now with the chimeras: the chimeras had red hair and had burst their ropes. They bounded up the stairway, crashed through the heavy doors leading from the deck, they were every creak and footstep on a ship soldered with creaks and footsteps. At last he picked up his suitcase and typewriter and struggled down the stairs back into his cabin. He lay there for fifteen minutes between the fat man's snores and the light from the passage, waiting for the citizen to dive through the curtain. Had there been a door to lock he might even have slept. He returned upstairs with his baggage and sat at the table. Soon a thin, dark man entered from below, nodded, and sat at the table.

—You were unable to sleep just now?

—What?

—I occupy the bed across from yours. Just now I heard you come in, and leave.

—I was attacked in the cabin not long ago. Perhaps you heard the noise. But then, you and the other are heavy sleepers.

—I saw the fight in the corridor.

—Fight?

—I saw you and the other. I thought it was a drunken quarrel, like the earlier one.

—That was not me earlier. That was someone else. I was asleep. I was attacked in bed.

—As I have heard. Are you badly hurt?

—I don't know.

—May I see? I am a doctor.

He tilted his head back and the doctor gently fingered the wound.

—It is not bad. It is not good, but not bad.

—There's a sharp pain in my ears.

—Can you hear?

—Yes.

—It is not serious.

—How did the fight begin?

—I don't know. I heard the sounds, got up, and saw you in the corridor.

The doctor remained a while longer, sympathetic, but shedding no light. At last the doctor excused himself. He passed the girl on the stairway.

"I can't sleep," she said. "I'd rather sit here with you."

"What time is it?"

"Half-past five. Two and a half more hours."

"If there was only something to drink . . ."

They missed the dawn. Morning came, passengers woke, dressed, gathered in the lounge to wait for the coffee that never came. He was the object of many stares, which he ignored. He was lucky to have the girl to seem to occupy him. The old steward told the story tirelessly, highlighting the eerie moans and the magnitude of the *mayordomo*'s blow.

"You look like you've been in a traffic accident," she said.

"Feel like it."

"You look very tough."

"I am. I should be dead now. Once, between the Canaries and Cadiz, he cut a man's throat."

"Who?"

"The madman on the boat. He makes every run."

"What?"

"You're losing your tan, Ingalill. Alicante will do you good."

"I'm afraid to stay in Alicante. I think we should go on to Valencia, or straight back to Barcelona."

"We'll stay awhile."

—How are you feeling? the guard said.

—As I look.

—You will not disembark with the rest. You will come first briefly to the vestibule to sign a complaint.

—May I finish my coffee?

—Of course. You are not a prisoner.

They were in Alicante. The morning sun poured into the harbor. Gray-green mountains rose behind the city. The *Jorge Segundo* must have radioed ahead, for scores of police and heavily armed *guardia civil* milled around at dockside. That was clever, he thought, *un franco vale* fifteen *pesetas, por lo menos;* they would certainly contain one wild man with that army.

A porter boarded the ship, advertising a third-class hotel. He sent the girl with the porter. Talking with the police and seeing the doctor might take some time. He took the name and address of the hotel and handed his typewriter to Ingalill. She followed the porter off the boat. He went to the captain's office in the stern, the area thickest with police.

The chief of police, a large, gentle man, presented him

with a document which he signed after a quick, fruitless attempt to read. He stood against the wall in the vestibule. To his right was the captain's office, where he could see the captain conferring with a gaudily dressed civil guard. From behind the curtain to his left issued unregenerate comments on the Iberian scene.

"*Arriba España, viva España,*" said the familiar voice, Up Spain. "*Franco! Franco! Franco! Vive de Gaulle.*" C——, c——, and l—— are components of the *guardia civil*. There was much of astrologic interest, and some whistling. He did not sound like a man with a broken nose. The two *guardia* who had, luckily, made the crossing, had been replaced by two others outside the cabin. The new pair exchanged smiles. He nodded, when one of them brought a circling finger to his three-cornered hat, indicating the state of the citizen's faculties. He had confronted the citizen for the last time in his waking life, and he did not wish it otherwise. But he wished he were invisible. Not to gloat, in order to believe. Hearing was believing, the presence of the police, his raw, tautening face, the moan that still sounded in his ears was believing, but he wanted to see, to inspect the trussed redhead one more time.

The citizen began to shout obscenely. One of the guards sadly shook his head, unslung his rifle, and entered the cabin. "*Hola!*" the citizen said. Hello and good night. There was no more noise. The guard stepped back into the vestibule. He smiled sheepishly. —He is asleep now, he said, "*El duerme bien.*"

A tap, a nap. In handling the criminal insane one meets the need for applied brutality. This is the murderous world now. It pays to befriend the law, as well as the madman. Smile often and be a good listener. Stay clear of politics. He was sick and tired, he wanted to see a doctor and go to the hotel. He accosted the chief of police.

—Do you need me here?

—No . . . no. How long will you be in Alicante?

—A day or two.

—Where will you be staying?

—Here. He produced the card he had taken from the porter.

—Good. I want nothing more from you. But you will have to speak briefly with the Civil Guard.

—Your passport, a tall, gray, uniformed man said, waggling his fingers. The *guardia* did not look at him. He fumbled in his jacket and trouser pockets for his passport.

—Come, your passport!

He produced it at last, and the man laboriously copied the information it held.

—The names of your parents.

—Charles Seth and Eve Lillian.

—You will write those here. How long have you known the man inside?

—I never saw him before the boat.

—That is not what he says.

—He is a madman.

—That is your opinion. He says you quarreled over a girl.

—There was no quarrel. I was asleep and he attacked me.

—That is not what he says.

—He is mad, the chief of police said. It is obvious.

—He is perhaps not so mad as he seems. He says he knows your sister.

His sister was nineteen now, a sophomore at Smith.

—It is a lie.

—So you say. We will find out, you can be sure. Go now.

—I'm waiting for the doctor. They said I would be taken to a doctor.

—Then wait for the doctor. Do as you please.

This led him to believe that there would be no doctor, let alone dry-cleaning or repair for the watch, but he waited for twenty minutes, standing on the deck apart from the thronging officials and ignoring stone-faced the workers and merchants who boarded the ship and stared at him frankly and curiously (although he had but recently revalued courtesy). A doctor came at last, to inspect the citizen. He emerged from the cabin and pronounced the citizen in good health. He held his breath, expecting the citizen to reappear, but he did not. When the doctor moved by him, down the gangplank, he decided to make his own way to a hospital. But the chief of police stopped the doctor, talked to him briefly, and the doctor turned and beckoned and led him to a taxi. A third man, a dock official, joined them. He had once been an ordinary seaman and traveled all over the world, he said, but particularly enjoyed New York. An old man with a smoker's cough, the doctor sat up front with the driver, smoking and saying nothing. He seemed bored. It was as the victim suspected; the citizen made every run, the doctor met every boat.

When they arrived at his office, the doctor clipped two metal prongs into his chin and covered them with gauze, free of charge. The dock official treated him to coffee in a nearby café. He ordered a croissant, he was very hungry, but he could not chew it. A short, dark man entered the café whom the dock official knew. One side of the man's face was completely hidden by bandages. The officer recounted the shipboard mishap to his friend. Where he lacked information, or seriously erred, the victim filled in. Told this way, the story had its lighter side, but the short man listened quietly with rising indignation.

—I would have killed him had he done it to me.

—I was asleep, he defended himself.

—That is the point. If he had woken me that way I would have killed him.

He shrugged. He put it down to hyperbole, the Latin temperament. But afterward, when he considered, it was the only line to take. He would murder the citizen the next time they met.

Taub East

A THOUSAND yards south of Fenollosa's grave is a granite gas chamber too seldom and casually used to instil much terror, and four hundred yards to the northeast, down out of the hills, lies a whitewashed chapel. This building is distinguished from fifteen others of similar appearance and size by the bronze crucifix rising thirty feet above the gabled doorway; also by proximity to the gym, the theater, and the service club. This last marks it as meant to see service during a leisure hour. The cluster of four buildings is separated from the workaday bulk of the camp by a closely cropped rectangular green, sometimes used as a parade field, and the whole nestles prim and swept at the foot of the tangled mountain. PX, bus depot, and BOQ lie across the road, escaping the orbit of the hills.

Dusk assaults Camp Hara as well as the town: charges

down from the mountain, rolls in from the lake, and out-
flanks the daylight. Spidery foliage and black rooftops take
on that diaphanous sheen recognizable from a thousand
paintings and sometimes confused with technique, but it is
something which happens to the air. Dusk covers the ex-
cursion boats moored at the lakeside pier, the high aluminum
dome which makes an arcade of Hama-Hara's shopping
street; it surrounds the radio tower and pummels the tiled
roof of the chapel (for all camp buildings are topped off in
local style); and dusk provides Taub a sign he relies on more
closely than on his almanac; so he turns from his fat lawyer
friend, Robert Helver, and clears his throat to greet the
Sabbath Bride.

He has now been abetting her unorthodox entry into Hara
for a little over a year.

Taub presides weekly with a poise and skill he once be-
grudged the congregation, not for being crumbs but lacking
always two to three crumbs of a *minyan*, the ten-man cachet.
One does not hold eight-man services in Hassidic circles,
nor even in Reformed; collects at least ten souls or regret-
fully, in time, disperses the flock to better-trafficked syna-
gogues. But the Army at home and abroad is not the Bronx
and the stylized tremolos he tickled from his chest, the
sweet falsetto moan he tortured from his throat, he tickled
and tortured (in any event) for the multitude: the unmarried and the undead and their relatives in heated temples
and by windswept tombs at the thousand wakes and wed-
dings that would one day turn upon his saucy baritone—
laboring incidentally for the seven men who face his back
this February night, restless eyes hindered by opaque saints
from mingling with the dusk, scratching gibbon sides and
waiting for the wine.

All the same, he is not undismayed; tonight as always he

had personally corralled the light-headed seven behind him, combing barracks and day room and service club in the weekly cajoling burlesque, the doomed dutiful attempt to convene ten or more. So he is fortunate that his complex theology permits him (in his mind) to make the adjustment required.

"*Boey vshalom*," boomed Taub, and revolved to face them as the prayer required. "The congregation will please rise," he inserted with almost too much unction for his own taste in the circumstances; he was impelled to smile sweetly at Helver, and at Popkin by his side.

"He sings very nice," said the older man.

"He sings very nice? Jesus. He's practically a rabbi."

"I know that," said Popkin. "We sleep in the same lousy room."

And only the anonymous five are in any way genuine. Popkin was purchased. Helver is his friend.

"The concluding prayer over the wine, page 217," acquired from my own pocket and what all you *gonifs* came for; let them sip from the silver cup wrought for his grandfather in a dead city named Vilna; all dynasties end.

"Nice service, Lyle," said a man returning to the Zone of the Interior next week, which is home. "Thank you I was a trifle off," said Taub. "Howbeit I'm glad you enjoyed."

He is no malcontent; though life is a patchwork of surprises. Through the early months he shaped events and became chaplain's assistant in Georgia. He made inroads into the substantial civilian community in those parts until one day he was shipped out, eight thousand miles from Atlanta. He began again from scratch before he discovered there was no Jewish chaplain at Hara for him to be assistant to. Himself was put in charge, an additional duty without privilege, basically rewarding but different from what he had in mind.

"Come again," Taub whispers after the retreating tribe. "Next week, champagne."

But dusk succumbs rapidly too; the lake suddenly mirrors the mountains (if there is a moon), and only the twinkle and shimmer from the officers' club, up in the hills, between the gas chamber and the scholar's grave, can disturb E. Fenollosa's remains. There is one more ghost to lay, that not so simple: within the camp itself, between mess hall and dispensary, on a slight rise in a treed-in enclosure which is off limits to all military personnel, is buried a brief-tenured, legitimate seventh-century emperor and this man is bathed in light—from the mess hall, the barracks, the bowling alley, and his is the greater irony: for Fenollosa lies at last within easy reach of his own color and kind.

From a synagogue on Friday night a man ordinarily goes home to the evening meal and the dutiful wife who has prepared it, but (it is worth repeating) we are a long way from home. A rare enlisted man wins, or wages, a battle with the mess hall, and Taub ate prior to his service between the daylight hours of five and six with the rest of the troops and did not feel put-upon. The snack bar stayed open nightly until ten-thirty, serving outrageous food at impossible prices, but by seven-twenty Taub was on the rocky convex road, bouncing round the familiar turning across which the great bent tree threw its shadow, older than the town itself; accompanied by Helver, directed toward a home, a hearth, the heart of a low strange city where the Sabbath never touched.

"Kazuko expects us," Helver said.

"That's excellent," sonorous still; the numinous feeling

ebbs slowly, confabulation with the Hebrew God. "And
how is the shackrat's dream?"

"I worry," says Helver, and it's clear he worries, in his
lardy, laughable body. "She's very possessive now, hardly
lets me go anywhere." He worries, puffed with pride, this
ugly, unlovable career man. Yet is he loved? No sweat,
regard the girl. From the pits of a society whose pits are
slimier than our own. She loves him? She gets more from
him each month than a professor receives in a year. So she
loves him. But irony, contempt, are misplaced here, Helver
is his friend.

"When is the wedding?" They moved past blind alleys,
tinsel cabarets; a sweet shop, an old man glimpsed through
a doorless doorway at a cobbler's last, gray hair cropped
close as Popkin's, over the ancient bridge, the putrid canal,
toward the house where Helver lived in sin with an animal
it was all too simple to explain. "When is the blessed event?"
pursues Taub.

"Who knows? It's not out of the question. I could do
worse, I already have."

This he claims, impossible to love or not: he has been
married before.

"You could," says Taub, but he does not believe it. This
pig has killed a man. In Washington, he was an MP then,
guarding a prisoner who reached into his pocket for a concealed weapon or a handkerchief (Helver tells this story on
himself). The criminal took eight slugs from a carbine set
on automatic in fleshy parts of the body, so face to the
ground clutched about in his pockets still; this wily wolf,
fangs lost in corpulence, reloaded in panic and pumped a
few more in the back of the head; emerged unjailed from a
court-martial but was transferred from the MPs to pursue the

law career for which Wisconsin U. had originally prepared him. Turned career man, stationed the past seven years in Japan.

". . . don't let her do the laundry. I take it to the quarter-master, I think she has enough work to do. So all that hap-pens is she gets suspicious, she thinks I'm keeping another girl."

Butcher! You're kind, don't let your *kourve* do the laun-dry? "I'll tell you a joke I just received from a friend in the States," says Taub. "It's nicely apropos."

Once a GI is sent home unexpectedly from overseas. He is a New Yorker of the Hebrew persuasion, who, on leaving the boat, phones up home.

—Hello, Mom? It's Joe. I'm in New York.

—Joe, you're really in New York? Discharged? You're not hurt? Come home!

—I'm on the way. Mom. There's just one thing I have to tell you first.

—What is it sweetheart?

—I'm married. I married a girl overseas.

—Married? You didn't even write about it. You married a girl overseas? Wonderful. Come home with the wife.

—There's just one more thing. My wife is a Japanese.

—Yes, in the papers, I read about it all the time. Lots of youngsters, they go abroad, they're lonely, they marry Japanese girls. But you're all right, Joey? Back from China, and not hurt or anything? That's all that matters.

—I'm fine, Mom. I was hoping you'd feel this way.

—How else is there to feel?

—We've got a baby, a year old, a little girl.

—Naturally. With marriage comes children, this is news? Ach, a grandmother. Who would believe it? Come home now Joey, the entire family.

—Swell, Mom, right away. I haven't much money, no plans as yet, we were hoping we could stay with you for a while.

—*Stay* with us? This is how you talk? This is your home. You live here as long as you like. You and the wife take your old room, Papa stays where he is, and the baby sleeps in your Mama's room. No problem will present itself.

—Sounds all right, Mom, for Mariko and myself . . .

—Mariko? Your wife? A *sheina* name!

—But if the baby sleeps in your bed, where will you sleep?

—Yussel, love, don't be concerned. When we disconnect I'm going to shoot myself.

Helver had a live one, come to him two years earlier with a bed and household goods (she never claimed to be a virgin). He was a sergeant even then, and they added PX mirrors and chairs and a blond bureau bought in town. Kazuko, to the bargain, had a decorative eye. Taub had long before conceded, it was pleasant for a shack, as distinct from Popkin's frayed-mat, nightsoil-smelling place near the camp (but Popkin lived with an attractive girl). Helver made no bones about it, he loved his happy home. Taub lived in the barracks (he was in fact his "room sergeant") because he happened to prefer it, but he understood the shackers (raunchy slobs, lonely swine). Helver chuckled.

"That's a very Jewish joke."

"No doubt," Taub said, unflurried by the compliment.

They ascended the almost vertical stairway and popped into the cozy room.

"Please to see you," offers Kazuko to her man's companion. She is over the hill all right, but has never seen better days. In her wrinkled brownie's face Taub sees that, all things being equal, native politeness will just barely cloak her fondest wish: that Helver had come home alone.

"You bring sackey, *ne!*" says Buddha, with acquired Eastern bluster; creases his short legs and drops to the floor. He loosens his belt so his monstrous belly tumbles free; Kazuko is no lightweight too. Image of elephants doing it, the poor bed at night. Taub regards it, condoles.

"And what's new at Finance?" Helver asks.

"Popkin came in for an advance on tomorrow's pay this afternoon, but I couldn't help him. Lieutenant Frick left explicit orders."

"I gave him five hundred tonight."

"Popkin?"

"Yeah. He put the bite on me before the service."

The girl returned from below with a tray bearing *sake*, cups, peanuts and peas.

"*Sake* is an acquired taste," says Taub, handling the word with elaborate care (Helver murders it). "I don't believe I have ever really acquired it." He elevates the cup.

"*Kampai*," he smiles, and clinks his own against Kazuko's thimble-sized cup.

"*Kampai*," she toasts, and grimaces in turn, though she is too dense to be impressed by his respect for the idiom, to observe how much he has absorbed, in a year, of the culture and the tongue.

"I think he's a bit paranoid," Helver breaks in on the scene; "he's got the idea Frick is sleeping with his girl."

"You know for a fact Frick isn't?"

"It's highly unlikely. He's just been reprimanded by the colonel, I happen to know, for making the EM bar and whore circuit. He's apt to be being careful."

"Ah? Well. If Frick isn't, someone else probably is. Popkin has no luck. Drunk, misfit, he's the backbone of the Army. He must continually suffer, official and off-duty pain. The military *must*, to function, crucify its own."

Thesis, and image, are equally bold. Kazuko, the *sake* poured, sits dully and regards the floor.

"Why you no talk?" Helver asks. "You bashful? You know Lyle long time, he good *tomodachi*. You very quiet tonight, don't you."

Now she shows her teeth, food and dull gold.

"The cat's got her tongue," says Taub. He undoes his belt, gives his own belly room. But he is not really enjoying himself. The couple swap infantile, rapturous smiles. Lord, the slut must be thirty-five, three years Helver's senior (eleven his own). A pig in any tongue. "So close to the end of the month," he says, "I wonder, is it quiet in town?"

"More sackey, *ne?*" Helver prods her gently and she moves to obey. But she looks reproachfully at Taub; more than reproach, almost the opposite of love. Well she divines the tenor of his last remark (and well he knows she does, the bitch, pariahs understand each other—he does not shrink from this explanation of their mutual perspicacity).

Well she is absent now (but not for long) and he makes his move.

"Did you mean to sit up here all night?"

"Yeah, why? You restless?"

"Come. Jackie's for a beer. Amusement by Akemichan."

"Don't really need it. Kaz will blow her stack. I haven't any yen anyway, to coin a phrase." But he can be had, Taub believes: he can spoil the scene for the fat man by expressing displeasure.

"A ball and chain," he jokes weightily, "God help you. Poor *lansman*, traded in his freedom for a piece of ass."

Helver grins. Such language costs Taub an effort, he knows; he thinks he feels something of the host's onus, too.

"Well, maybe for a quick drink. If Kaz will lend me the yen. She doesn't like me out on the town."

"Naturally not," says Taub.

Up the stairs burdened by refreshments comes the ample peasant girl, barefoot, looking great from behind. Neither subtle nor delightful, she clatters the tray onto the low table, and only once in the next ten minutes will her black deadly eyes light on Taub.

"You go downtown?"

"Ears in the back of her head," says Helver, with an owner's love. "Yes honey, maybe I go with buddy catch one beer. Okay, *ne,* come back home soon. No have Japanese money, you lend me thousand yen, okay?"

"My no have," she says brightly. She will certainly use this unexpected luck.

"I could spare a hundred," Taub says doubtfully.

"Honey, you lie to me," Helver says gravely. "Yesterday I give you three thousand, impossible you already spend. You tell lie, I think. Lend me one thousand yen now, *ne!*"

"Why you want drink bar? Have plenty drink in house. I can go buy more."

Inviting praise, Helver cocks a brow at Taub; she's right, you know. "Kaz," he says, "no have to worry. *Shimpai nai.* You think I go whorehouse? That is what you think, *ne?* Never happen. I go have one drink cabaret, come back home."

"Why you want thousan, beer price hunner eighty. You go bar, I can go too."

"That would change the picture," laughs Taub, and it is here she nails him with her brilliant blackeyed rage.

"*Go men nasai,*" he says—he is more shaken than he shows. "But you must be aware of the feelings toward other females of the girls who work in bars."

"You give me five hundred yen," says Helver. "Maybe

want drink *two* beers. *Hayaku!* I no go whorehouse, honey, honest to god. Only go have lousy beer."

A snicker comes from Taub.

Involving (she knows) Buddha's pride. "You come home soon?" she says bitterly.

"Honey you know it," Helver replies.

From her bosom she extracts a brown roll of notes from which she peels four which Helver presses to his lips, then counts. The girl anticipates: "Four hundred yen enough you can buy two beers." Helver is really touched by this. "Honey," he says, "you can give me four *thousand* yen, I no never go whorehouse."

Cumulative sentiment and syntax prove too much for Taub. "*Ojama shimashita,*" he says roundly, and makes to depart; he even bows a little. He has learned the right formulae in his time (he owns a text called *Japanese in a Hurry*), and truly, he thinks, he has committed a nuisance by luring her mate to face the ripe temptations of Hara's nighttime world. Poor girl, she is also luckless, he commiserates; shoeshiner for the Outcasts, awrily matched against their king.

On the cool road, under a sometime moon:

"Let me say this, Bob. She'll never learn English if you also use that horrible pidgin. Speak correctly, she'll start to do so too."

"Maybe," Helver grins. "But who knows how long we're going to live?"

2

The five hundred yen in PFC Popkin's pocket when he left the chapel that night was that much more than he thought he would need. While there was nothing he wanted to buy, an empty wallet made him feel naked, or out of uniform. That was why he applied for an advance at the Finance Office, that was also why he was refused. With the loss of three stripes and one hundred fifty dollars went certain less obvious humiliations. They knew what they were doing. After twenty-one years with the Army, three court-martials and countless instances of company punishment, Popkin knew what they were doing too. With Helver's help he thwarted them. They might bust him and levy a fine; they could not leave him naked while he still had a friend.

Popkin was fond of wine. Wine frequently undid him, but he learned nothing from punishment. He needed no capital tonight to satisfy his thirst, piqued pleasantly by the toast in the chapel. Three bottles of Akadama, a cheap port-type native brew, were stored beneath his and Reiko's bed, in the house along the blind dirt road which formed Camp Hara's northern boundary. He moved now toward this hoard, through the ragged gap in the wire fence behind the service club.

He felt no pain. The lake banked in to a point thirty yards from where he passed, and he sniffed the night air, rising to combat the dungy odors of the daylight. Out of the star-pricked sky that canopied the foreign night the Big Dipper rushed to meet him, balanced crazily on its head, like a man's close friend he has never seen drunk before. A PFC at forty-five, he was his own man still, in a strange, peacetime world. Up the road he had his grape and girl. Life was definitely bearable. On impulse, he retraced a few yards to a small shop. With the five hundred yen he bought a bottle of Ocean Whiskey, which he stuffed into his back pocket. Reiko didn't drink much, but liked whiskey when she did. So there was the borrowed money now, doing considerably more than soothing his pride; there was never a time when you couldn't hit on something useful to buy. The whiskey would be a peace offering. He wouldn't hand it over right away. First he would evoke the impassioned denials concerning her and Lieutenant Frick, only this time he would decide to believe her.

The house was in a clearing behind the road, led to by a narrow lane. It was ancient, smelly, in disrepair, but stocked for him with six months of memories. At the mouth of the alley squatted their neighbor, an old woman, blocking his passage, her kimono up about her ears. She ignored him until she was done. Then she struggled upright and clutched his arm.

"*Reichan iahen yo.*" Her face worked wildly. "*Gō Kyoto tempurr.*"

"That's all right, so's you don't wet yourself." He pulled free and continued down the alley. The dark, sealed hulk lopped the warmth from him, a scythe-stroke he could almost hear.

She was not home. He had left his key inside. He drew close and yanked on the padlock, without hope. She knew his Friday schedule, she should have been home. He dropped onto a tree stump a few yards from the door. He knew he was wasting his time: if she was only shopping, or

at the restaurant, she would not have locked up so completely, would have left a light burning inside. All the same
he'd sit and wait a quarter of an hour.

The woman approached and gripped his arm. She croaked,
"*Tempurr, tempurr.*" She gestured vaguely toward the hills.
She had something on her mind but he could not be bothered
by her. She spoke no English, she was impossibly old.
"Temper, temper," he aped. "Easy to give advice. But she
ought to be home."

"*Osō made kaette kiahen wa. Mattara akan.*" She grimaced;
without teeth, or context, Popkin took it as a smile. He returned it. He took off his steel-rimmed spectacles, ran over
the lenses with a khaki handkerchief. The whiskey made sitting uncomfortable. He drew it from his pocket. If there
had been a way to get in the house, at the wine, he would
not have minded this so much. He spun the bottle in his
hand, ripped off the wrapping, and unscrewed the cap. He
took a long pull. He wiped the neck with the handkerchief
and handed the bottle to the woman, who squatted beside
him.

She waved her hand in front of her face. "*Mamasan
nomahen.*"

"Just this once. A special favor. Don't make me drink
this crud alone."

"*Sukoshi itadakimasu.*" She received the bottle in two
withered hands and raised it to her mouth. "*Oishikatta,*" she
said, returning it. Her finger went to the single strip of cloth
at his elbow; she tentatively brushed his steely crop.
"*Kawaisō da, na,*" she said.

"No sweat, lady," Popkin said. "I've been better before.
That's the story of my life in fact. I shuttle between private,
sergeant first class."

"No spiku inlis," the old woman said.

"Maybe so," Popkin said. "But this time was different from the other times. It ain't that I was drunk on duty, I just never came in. I was completely covered so far as I knew. It was a midweek midnight shift, maybe three messages will arrive, nothin' goes out. Nance agrees to handle it all, the corporal, if I give him off next time we share mids. Naturally. I stay shacked and I rest up and drink my wine.

"So guess who is in the officers' club till two a.m.? Yessir, my buddy Frick, sir. Plastered. Has a terrible urge to shoot the shit with the midnight crew, though he has never turned up after five-thirty before. Naturally he wants the tricks chief, Nance says I'm out for coffee. He waits. He sobers up. Boom, an AWOL charge."

"*Mō sukoshi kuremahen ka?*"

"What? This? *Dōzo*. Don't look like there's much left to celebrate tonight." He gave her the whiskey, took it back and drank himself. It scorched his throat, burned his belly, but was better than nothing at all.

"A special court. Not even a warning first. My first offense in this country, and I got my last two stripes in frozen Chosen. (Our playboy friend has never been to Korea.) Busted almost all the way down. They don't even transfer me after. Hara needs its signal personnel; Frick don't know ass from elbow. Son of a bitch. Reiko's friend."

She recalled her charge. "*Reichan kiahen wa,*" she whined. "*Gō Kyoto tempurr.*"

"I don't know," Popkin said. "Naturally, she denies it. I was ready to believe her. But if she ain't with him tonight, where in hell can she be?"

The night he told her he was a PFC Reiko hit him, that was how mad she was. "You a crazy old man! No care about me, about Army, only care about wine."

"Now simmer down and take it easy. . . ."

"Take it easy? You like someone take it easy you better catch other girl."

"It wasn't my fault. He didn't have to do it. I know for a fact now there was no traffic that night. He was drunk, he had to feel his balls."

"Lutenan Frick do his job. When sergeant suppose to go work, he go work. Not tell lie about night off, stay with me, get stinko, make love. If now I go catch lutenan only one night, make more money, *deshō*, than stay one month with you."

"Try it."

"I no scared of you. You think I scared? I know him longer time than you, many time he come see me when I work in Pedro's bar."

"So you and he . . ."

"I know him long time before meet you," she said. "He not happy with wife, come Pedro's bar. Why? You worry now? If still SFC, not PFC, no have to worry. Now I must make money some way. So some night you know why you come back here I not be home. . . ."

He damn well remembered this threat, she'd made it good, and all the tears and denials in between made no difference. She was out with Frick, "making money" tonight. A risky conclusion, he'd check it first. He corked the bottle, about half full, and stuffed it into his pocket.

"Excuse me. I might be back. I have a call to make."

He walked back through the ruined fence and into the service club. He dialed Dependents Housing. "Connect me with Lieutenant Frick's residence," he said.

A worried voice rasped in his ear, the john's gawky wife. "I'd like to speak to the lieutenant, please."

"I'm sorry, he's not in. Is there a message?"

"Uh no. Nothin' printable." He hung up the phone.

In the service club a horsey hostess with a portable mike led the troops and their friends through bingo. Most of the players were men of the bottom three grades. He looked over the shoulder of a private he knew. As SFC he had shared a room with two others, with a houseboy to keep things tidy. The sergeants avoided bedcheck, and escaped most Saturday inspections. Now, he lived in a roomful of privates and PFCs. The household chores, the palaver of draftees, did not shake him up as much as one a.m. bedcheck, rigidly enforced by Taub, threatened to. If he and Taub had not finally worked this out between them, no knowing what would have happened to his home life, up the road.

But that was all fouled up anyway. His phone call did not exactly prove that Reiko was with Frick—but one more piece dropped into place. They were probably holed up in one of Hara's thousand cheap hotels, or maybe even further afield in the plush Kyoto Hotel. Or maybe they were not. In the end, she had only gone shopping, or visiting, and she was home waiting for him now. While he spent time twisting the knife kibitzing a bingo game. He started back for the house, the liquor taking hold, having one more pull at the start of the alleyway; remembering still why he had bought it but at once sickeningly certain he would not find her home.

It seemed the old lady had not moved in all this time. She squatted in the same position, her hands on the stump. She looked up as he approached. She was, he could tell, even drunker than he was, and he scolded her, to keep his thoughts from the bleak house behind.

"You're crocked. Don't think I ought to let you have no more."

"*Anta mada hayai zo,*" she reproved in turn. "*Sonna ni hayō kaette kiehen. Kitto jū ni ji made go tempurr.*"

"Jews need nothing," he said, "that somebody else don't

need as well. That's from the horse's mouth, I'm half-Jewish myself. The rabbi though is a special case. He needs one extra thing, bodies. Hey, you know this story?" For she scratched her head, rose, and walked away. "*Chotto matte, ne,*" she called.

"Sure," he said; he understood this phrase. "I ain't goin nowhere."

The Popkins had Taub over for dinner the day Taub hinted at a way round bedcheck, more from perversity than gratitude. Taub was a crud; the Army were worse cruds; Taub might give him a chance to get back at the Army. To order Reiko to produce a meal on short notice was part of it too: if the house was crumbling he was still its master, he could still bring an honored buddy home for chow.

"Superb *sukiyaki*," Taub had said. "She can cook to the bargain."

"What do you mean, to the bargain?"

"I mean she's a fine-looking woman, hardly run-of-the-mill."

"Yeh. About bedcheck, what's on your mind?"

"You understand my position. I'm in charge of the room. I must see to it that it's ready for inspection, I must hand in a list of all parties not in bed by one. Needless to say, I don't relish the job, I certainly didn't request it. Personally, I couldn't care less who does what all night, but I'm forced to protect myself. If a man's name is missing from the bed-check list and he is afterwards apprehended off the post, or if Beddoes or the captain pull a surprise check at four a.m., my ass is personally in the sling."

"It's a tough life."

"That may be. You know, I consider it a shame about your court-martial. Absolutely uncalled for."

"That's the truth."

"Company punishment perhaps, maybe the loss of a stripe, but not broken to PFC and then having to pay a fine."

"Miscarriage of justice," said Popkin, not anxious to discuss it with this chickenshit two-year man.

"You're Jewish, aren't you."

"On my father's side."

"On your father's side. Forgive my asking: do you think of yourself as a Jew?"

"What's the angle?"

"I'm thinking of sticking my neck out. If you're qualified and interested. I conduct Jewish services on the post, as you might know. The attendance is poor, despite the fact that twenty or more Jews are stationed on the post, and I'd like to increase it."

"I've never been to a service."

"No time like the present. If you care to attend, I guarantee the name Popkin never appears on the bedcheck list. You work in Signal, at odd hours: I need only say, if they check, I thought you had duty that night. It's a risk I'm willing to take in exchange for one hour a week of your time. You could return here each night to your charming girl as you're accustomed to."

"I'd be honored to attend the Jewish service," Popkin said.

"Superb. You might even find it rewarding." He looked at Reiko, bent over the stove. Her coal hair down her face, her rear etched against the PX navy blue. "I assume you know that Lieutenant Frick, while married, runs around in town."

"I've heard about this.

"His persecution of you," Taub went on. "I wonder if it's gratuitous, or stems from resentment that an EM lives with such a lovely girl. Could there be, frankly, anti-

Semitism involved. But listen, however that may be: if my immediate superior were a vindictive *vonce* like Frick, and to the bargain I lived with a *shtik fleish* like yours, I'd keep up my guard."

"Maybe," Popkin said. He tried to drum up some warmth for Taub. He knew no Yiddish, supposed Taub did him a favor by assuming he did. Still, the drift was clear. It echoed his private suspicions. He'd make good use of the time he gained.

And he did. By attending the service four weeks running, he was able to sleep with Reiko three nights out of every four, excepting the one when he went to work at midnight. So he was three-quarters sure that, despite her early, since-repudiated threat, she had not tried to screw him, with Frick or anybody. Yet he made her sweat the twenty-five per cent, the nagging doubts, until he bought the whiskey tonight on borrowed money to announce the reconciliation. And she wasn't home.

"*Kore mi na,*" the old woman said. She held a flashlight and a photograph, the photo bright before his eyes. Popkin focused on a Buddhist temple. "Very nice. A house of worship. I have just come myself from the synagogue."

"*Reichan tempurr e ikahatta,*" she said. "*Otōsan shinda kara.*"

"You want a drink?" But she thrust the bottle away.

"*Bakayarō!*" she croaked, when he brought the bottle to his lips. "*Baka!*" she yelled, and held the picture, the light, a few inches from his nose. Popkin pushed them away. "You're mad as a loon," he said gently. "You've had a hard life. I need to take a little walk." He pushed off from the stump and staggered to the road, turned off it onto the main road which split Camp Hara in two. He made his way in toward the town.

3

We seek a wraith through Hara's dowdy night with the morals of a maniac; luckier than she, we mean her no harm. Akemi Yamada is her name, Shiga her birthplace, she's spindle-thin with the face (says Taub) of an angel; he means by this she resembles the petite Miss Rheingold of a recent year. But this is no merely cute, exotic night-child; this is much more than an ill-starred *objet d'art*. Akemi is wit and raconteur, and these are the aspects that lure him. She represents his only link with the GI-Japanese underworld.

What Taub doesn't know, or admit, is that her friends fall into two categories even if he withholds his appreciation: these have included, at their extremes, the rotund Korean doyen of an Osaka dope ring, and a U.S. major with a degree on the arts side from Cornell. (There's an overlap, too: she has been known to vamp the high IQs and she can entertain, if she chooses, almost anyone across a table.) He's unaware of this, or overlooks it anyway. To his mind only he strains past her lecherous frailty to glimpse the queen behind; the *kourve* is a Dorothy Parker at times. With her doings after closing, for bread or kicks, he's unconcerned. This is between herself, and the cops, and her imported pagan gods.

On her part Akemi is all heart and half curiosity; there's space in her ridiculous bosom for Taub. In her time she has known variations, subtle and not, on almost every attitude, but she has never before been patronized. This is why she permits, occasionally even encourages, his generosity and attention—so long as the bar is not full, and she is not in conversation with a blond, twentyish member of the Military Police (of which there are several at Hara, with whom she is collectively and seriously in love)—on those infrequent occasions when Taub stops by. He buys her a screwdriver, beer for himself, and they shoot the breeze; she flies off *sans* ceremony when her drink is gone, when others arrive, or if she is not being entertained. Generally, Taub is unperturbed by her frank (if un-Japanese) rudeness. He knows she is the only employee at Jackie's Bar whose drinks are not watered (this is by her own request), and too much alcohol usually brings out the worst in people. So that while he counts drinking among the milder of her aberrations, he allows it to explain the volatile nature of their urbane, innocent, cerebral affair.

He knows a thing or two more. Unmarked by countless crises, a life of continual debauch, she will look twenty when closer to twice that age, but the fact is that in February 1954 (this data can be checked at the Judge Advocate's Office) Akemi has just put her twenty-eighth birthday behind.

"I am terribly sorry, no. Not one is immune. It's simply a matter of degree, and three cover the field."

"I doubt that," Helver said. "Suppose we consider . . ."

"Now listen to me a second. You'll cite exceptions? Do so. I say only this. That everyone you want to mention fits into Category Three. In this group you find it deep, perhaps it never surfaces. Such people might live a lifetime voting the liberal ticket, calling your attention to Einstein and Freud; they're not even aware they loathe the Jews. That's perhaps a trifle strong, maybe not *loathe*, but they know him to be in their hearts a lower form of life. So when Freud turns up it amounts almost to mutation, you cite the case to show how unbigoted you are. These people are as guilty as the rest."

Helver shook his head. "You leave no space for argument."

"Exactly the point. Let's proceed to Group Two, where feelings are nearer the surface, but still unimplemented without outside aid. They are waiting for Hitler. They need a leader to confirm them: not only is the Jew a lower form of life, he is an evil force. Thank God in our country there has been nothing quite like that up to now, but this breed of *goyim* says, McCarthy? G. L. K. Smith? This is a free country, Ikey, they have rights to their opinions too. Sure. As thieves have to steal, murderers to kill. About the third group, even you don't want to debate. Here are the active *anti-Semiten*, who murder you. The *momsers* who implement their hate, cause the real, not merely subtle distress. Am I wrong?"

"Things all over have been worse than they are."

"And *last*, we have the group which is in some ways worst of all, the anti-Semite Jews. But this of course is a class apart from the main stream."

"You mean me?"

"No no you have guilt feelings?" Taub clapped the back of the gross, good-natured man; in a hostile world, it is good to be with a friend.

Even with one so refractory; for where else lies the meaning of friendship? His good qualities are many, but he is not precisely an intellect, Helver, he has not breathed four years running the heady involuted air of the highest-priced college in New York. Taub is warm and compassionate as they near Jackie's Bar. The skinny sprite waits ahead, the depressing scene, the lumpish Kazuko, have been shunted behind.

"It follows," the lawyer persists, "that the Japanese are anti-Semites too."

"You think not? Permit an illustration. I was having coffee in the snack bar the other day with Nakamura, who works over at Finance. He's a *Tōdai*—Tokyo University—graduate, fairly bright. He wants to buy a house. He goes to an agent. The agent asks too much. Nakamura says, 'I tried to jew him down.' Now what are you bursting to say: merely an expression he picked up on post, doesn't even know what it means? I say you're wrong. I say, even if you're right, it won't be long before he finds out what it means, and I guarantee his attitude to me will alter when he learns I'm Jewish, if his knowing this was not why he made the remark in the first place. All prejudice is learned. Here they know the American white thinks Asians are inferior, they resent it. Yet they admire and envy the white man. They jump at the chance to take over his outgroups. They already hate blacks, you know. When it comes to bigotry, we have nothing to teach the sons and daughters of Amaterasu. You know what they feel toward Koreans, and their own so-called outcast class, the *eta;* all they need do is read a history of anti-Semitism in the West, they'll adapt quick enough."

"So you modify the original proposition. All non-Jews do not hate the Jews by definition. First they have to hear about them. The Buddhist and Hindu worlds are still only potential."

"Hairsplitter!" booms Taub affectionately. "You'll make a good shyster lawyer someday."

The bar was just beneath the arcade, at the mouth of the main shopping street, invisible behind a restaurant which was sandwiched between a haberdasher and a *geta* shop. A narrow corridor to the left of the restaurant led back to the bar. Jackie was a fortyish fullback of a woman who had it both ways. She did a roaring shoppers' trade up front in daylight hours (and lured the movie crowd at night), and the rear cabaret was one of the most popular GI spots in town. As our warriors near this site, their alien parley lost amidst the squawks and murmurs of oblivious passers-by, they're hailed by a countryman, concealed in a knot of bedizened strollers some way up the road. He's merely among them, not of them, breaks through presently with shaky strides, hatless, khaki-clad, no taller than the population at large.

"What's the action?"

"You're drunk, Lester," Helver says. "You're out of uniform."

"I mean besides that," Popkin says. "You join the MPs?"

"No, look. It was a special court. I did better than I should have keeping you out of jail. You shouldn't take chances so soon. Why don't you stay at home?"

"You know," says Taub, for the man's own good, "you endanger me too."

"Christ, is it one a.m.?" He checks his watch, with aghast, elaborate civility.

Helver says, "Put your hat on at least. It would be dumb to get picked up for something like that. Do you have to be out tonight?"

"Bob, I tell you honestly, I would rather be home. I would much rather be home. But I can't get in the goddamn house. Nobody home. I have the idea she's laying Frick, what's your opinion of that idea?"

"Now Pop," Helver says. "We've discussed this before.

Every troop with a shack has a similar idea. I have it myself sometimes. It's an occupational hazard."

"You mean you don't think she is."

"No."

"Frick ain't home."

"Very likely. As usual, he's at the officers' club. Look, we're going in here for a drink. Come along."

"To chat," adds Taub, "with the witty Akemichan. Nothing more ambitious is contemplated. Do you know Akemi?"

"Know her? I fucked her. Long time ago when I was still a free agent. Much too skinny for my taste."

To Helver, Taub says, "Shall we proceed inside?"

"Proceed," Popkin says. "Enjoy hell out of yourself. I'm going home like Bob suggests. Perhaps developments. Toodleloo."

He dons the hat; he lurches on. From his back pocket the bottle protrudes. "He'll find trouble," Helver says. "Or it him."

"I hope you're wrong," says Taub. "The unhappy slob."

Thirteen hours to payday—the service club is full tonight, there are very few troops in town. Jackie is up front among the Japanese, and only a girl named Tomiko, on duty since the afternoon, decorates the gloom behind. As they enter she puts aside her *True Story* in translation and flicks on the colored lights and the phonograph. The noisy hybrid of hillbilly and rock-and-roll elicits from Taub an involved cross between a pout and a frown.

"Please!" he yells. "No music, please."

The girl looks shocked, but complies. She flops over leisurely, rests her knuckles on the table. "You want two beer?"

"If it's not too much trouble. Two Kirin, please."

She goes to the bar and returns with the beer.

Taub asks: "Where's Akemi?"

"Come later maybe eight ten o'clock. Too early now. Maybe no come."

"*Yasumi ka?*"

"What you say?"

So she ruins herself: that close to being requested to partake, to sit with the pair.

"I said," said Taub, " '*Yasumi ka?*', which translated from the original yields the meaning, Is it her day off?" He's infuriated when they pretend not to understand. His grammar is passable, his accent fair. They treat their language like a sacred cow, the outsider cannot touch.

"*Ah so*, you say '*Yasumi ka.*' No, not today, but sometime end of month she go way, no come till late," and she flashes a ribald, toothy smile.

"I see," he says, indulging the rare impulse to judge this undelicate and (when all is said) chief side of Akemichan.

After pouring their beer she says, "May I sit down?"

"No!" Taub snaps, but fabricates, "*Yōji ga arimasu kara* . . . we want to talk."

"Shit," she says, and shuffles back to her magazine.

"A delicate creature," says Taub.

Helver shrugs. "What's so pressing to talk about?"

"You have funds?"

"Two-twenty yen."

"Ah. Nor am I a millionaire. If she sits, she must be entertained. When Akemi comes in, I'm out the price of a screwdriver. Call the *tuchess* back if you want to underwrite her."

"You go for Akemi in a big way," Helver says.

"It's platonic," Taub begins, but sees he is twitted by the fat man. "Oh yes," he says. "Why not a double wedding in the spring."

"Your pass was approved, I saw it in the orderly room. Where you headed for?"

"The Inland Sea. One of the beauty spots I've missed. It's easy to grow fond of this country. A man does not learn much by sleeping with a nation's prostitutes, despite the theory to the contrary."

"Never heard of that one."

"Come now. You've been here five years. You know the military mind. Surely . . ." but he's cut off: a tremulous love song floats down the corridor (at times Taub is struck by the similarity between certain Japanese and Hebrew melodies, as well as techniques of voice control; could they be after all, as a closely written book in the post library suggests, the Thirteenth Lost Tribe?), and the clack of *geta*, and Akemi, flushed and lovely, stands in the doorway. She wears a red sweater, a tartan skirt, and her legs are bare over the clogs. She's not herself; she's herself rather plus hemp, liquor, or both. She's giggly, and her eyes are on fire.

"*Ohayō*," Tomiko greets her. "*Kaerusan ga iru*," and returns to the magazine. The sprite squints into the gloom, and locates Taub. "Ah, *Kaeru*," she says (which never ceases to annoy: why, even in jest, he does not resemble one, does she call him Mr. Frog?). "*Comment ça va?*"

"*Ça va*," says Taub, and he thinks that this exchange, in spite of all, establishes the proper mood. He has taught it to her himself.

Yet she flits past their booth and drops down next to Tomiko.

"*Kita?*"

"*Dare ga?*"

"*Karwairashii* MP, *kinō kita no.*"

"*Mada kiahen.*"

"*Kuso!*" says Akemi, and stamps on the floor.

"Dung!" translates Taub. "My cute MP has not yet been in tonight."

Akemi turns. "*Wakatta?*" she says, with only half-feigned admiration. "You understand like native, no can say nothing round here."

She knows the tortuous route to the cantor's buttressed heart.

"I get by," says Taub. "Come and join us for the usual."

"Need a double tonight," Akemi says.

"A double! Well all right then. And bring us two more Kirin beers."

"*Arigatō,*" she replies. She pours a glassful of vodka (Jackie is up front, the bartender is late), opens the beer, and joins the pair.

"What did you do today," asks Taub, "to make you look so fiery-eyed?"

She giggles self-indulgently. "*Tsumaranai koto:* not worth your attention."

"Doubtless; who with?"

"*Nan da*, don't worry your fat head," and pats him on the crown. "Too much grease," she decides, but he grabs her hand before she wipes it on his trousers.

"You're *taihen* rude tonight," he scolds; she's so much more than this she's nearly out of hand. "Perhaps you shouldn't drink any more."

"This is first drink I have all day," she says to Helver. "Skinpop." She flexes her skinny arm.

"They'll slap you in jail again," Helver says.

"No skin from your nose, *Debuchan*. Anyway, no GI

involved." She has met the lawyer in his professional capacity before. She laughs wildly.

"You know what I do today? I make love in Blue Sky Hotel. First time this year."

This surprises Helver (a hotel in the environs of which he has not heard?) and depresses Taub; he has heard the bit before.

But Helver asks, "Where's the Blue Sky Hotel?"

Her head arches, she laughs like a child.

"She refers to the great outdoors," inserts Taub. "Like beasts, in bushes, under trees. It's her notion of a joke I believe." He lofts his beer.

"I see," Akemi says, "you not in very good mood tonight."

"I'm fine," he assures her; he has seen the possibility of four hunded yen disappearing with total lack of recompense. "But I have heard that joke before."

"You *takusan* egoist. You never think of other people."

"I apologize, Akemi. From now on I will think of other people."

"In a pig's ass," she says.

Helver, wittingly, delays catastrophe: "Your English has improved, Akemi."

"Thank you," she says, really pleased. "Only rude, broken GI English I learn working here, but sometimes study on the side."

"What are you reading these days, Akemi?" Taub labors to keep them on the firmer ground.

"Reading *ka!* I read Shakespeare *no Hamuretto*," and she is tickled by the affinities this has with "omelet" in the Japanese. Her laugh once more dances through the clubby darkness, then burbles into the vodka, which she is drinking straight. She has never been quite this far out in Taub's memory; the evening, he fears, will not be a success. He talks to Helver: "I was strolling in the hills behind the camp the other day, and I came across something interesting."

"What did you came across?" Akemi pounces on his lead—immediately she yells at Tomiko, "Phonograph *kakete kurehen?*" Tomi does, and the strident sounds once more fill the room.

"A grave," shouts Taub. "This man Fenollosa, very interested in Japanese art. The Japanese government sent a warship to pick up his body when he died. I had no idea he was buried here. *Gaijin no gakusha no haka o mitsuketa,*" he adds, so she too may understand.

"Never heard of him," mumbles Helver, staring hard at Akemi, who sits across from him adjoining Taub.

"Admired by Ezra Pound," Taub says. "But we needn't hold that against him. Need we." He turns to smile broadly at Akemichan.

Who has rolled up her sweater, unhooked her brassiere, and is studying a tiny breast. "*Okashii, na,*" she says with wonderment.

Taub's jaw drops, his body recoils.

"What in God's name are you up to now?"

"Very odd," she says. "Since week ago I find here something look like milk, there is no reason for. *Kore goran,*" she orders, turns, makes the bub convenient to the cantor's eyes. Helver leans forward. She applies pressure. A cloudy liquid appears. She looks amazed. "*Hen da, ne,*" she says to Helver, whose mien accords.

"What you think of that?" she says to Taub. "I have milk, but no damn babysan."

Jackie now enters the bar, counterfeits horror at the tableau, and goes to talk with Tomiko.

"We must go," Taub starts to rise. "She's not herself tonight."

"Where you off to?" She smiles suddenly at a secret thought, scratches her bare belly.

"I, back to camp." He looks at Helver. "Come."

"Okay, I'll make it back too. Kaz will be pleasantly surprised."

"Why you running off, *Kaerusan*," she repeats, but still does not sound awfully concerned.

"Because," Taub says slowly, "you are behaving like an ill-mannered slut tonight."

"*Hommae*, that's me all over." She drops the sweater and glances at Jackie, who has placed her stout frame behind the bar. This, she realizes, cuts off her illegal liquor supply. "Before you go you buy me one more vodka, *nee*. It just now begins to feel real good."

"Sorry," says Taub.

"Don't be *kechinbō*," she enjoins. "Next time you come in I buy you a drink. *Katte okure, Kaerusan*."

"I'm sorry, if you'll let me get by."

"Certainly." She slides her legs to the side of the bench, giving him room. As he inches past she yanks at the seat of his trousers. "Buy me drink, corporal make good pay."

"Out of the question," says Taub.

"Go to hell," she says without rancor. "You a cheap stingy Jew."

Helver is almost to the door, but he turns at this, sees Taub lumber about and lift his hand. Christ he'll hit her, he thinks; he already envisions the trial.

"Now you *shut up!*" Taub croaks. "You *whore*, just keep your mouth closed." His face is different shades of pale beneath the overhead revolving rainbow. Helver starts back but Taub drops his hand, moves past Helver and down the corridor.

"*Sayonara. Odaiji ni!*" Akemi calls, through immediately forgotten surprise. But she has had a quick vision of meaning in the world. She giggles softly, looks dolefully at Jackie. With sudden hope she peers down the corridor, but no MPs, blond or otherwise, are in sight. If one or another of them fails to appear, or anyone else, which is possible, the evening threatens dry, unspeakable boredom. To turn her mind from this she rolls up her sweater, and once more scrutinizes the mystery fluid she loves to squeeze from her pageboy's supple barren form.

As a gesture of solidarity and probably superfluous caution, Helver accompanied Taub from the door of Jackie's to Camp Hara's snack bar, where coffee and cheese on rye, and a buoying piece of inside intelligence, restored Taub to something like pre-Akemi form. Helver divulged that the post commander had decided to run HQ Company the following morning through the gas chamber up in the hills. This was in line with a standing order to keep chairborne Far East troops on a nodding acquaintance with combat conditions. All men below the rank of sergeant would mask; enter, by twos, the fume-filled chamber; make their way to a point near the exit where the first sergeant waited; remove masks, recite name rank and serial number; stagger out into the air. Helver's rating spared him; Taub would evade the small ordeal by means of his three-day pass.

The cantor safe, Helver started homeward, choosing a route through the back streets of the town. More than an hour had passed since the pair left the bar. He walked slowly past the small silent cluster of moonlit brick dwell-

ings of Hama-Hara's well-to-do, from here to the one street
which was its pleasure quarter, the row of shops and bars
and houses seeming to have sucked in the noise and population of the surrounding countryside, past it to the decrepit
bridge, pressing himself to the railing as the big Army bus
lumbered by. He did not trouble to unfreeze, although he
could have left the narrow bridge in time. The white convertible was thirty yards to the rear of the bus and not moving fast. Laziness kept him there, astonishment drove it out;
the split-second panic when the car came toward him, for
him, fled in turn before the reflexes that once, in Washington, D.C., had been too quick for all concerned: he was able
to reach over the driver's chest after saving himself and grab
futilely at the wheel. The car was committed by then. He
watched it smash the rail, dive with massive grace into the
shallow canal. He rushed to the earth embankment and waded
into the stew. For some moments (just long enough) he was
the only other person on the scene.

4

While not the world's most serious Buddhist, making peace
with piety in general by infrequent trips to *Inari*, patron
goddess of the working girl, Reiko felt moved to leave Hara
on the seventh anniversary of her father's death and visit the
family temple. Her mother dunned her by letter for the six
weeks preceding the day, but she might have remembered
anyway. She had behaved badly since his death, working in
bars and cabarets, contracting unsavory relationships with
GIs from her native Kyoto to as far south as Beppu, and this
propitiatory gesture to her father's ghost and her mother's

anxiety made good sense, since she lived now no more than an hour's ride from where she was born. The round trip to Kyoto, in all, should have taken under five hours.

She knew well in advance she would make the journey, but she put off telling Popkin when their trouble came. The old *sukebei* would not have believed her. On the morning of the day she thought she noticed a softening in his attitude, but was unwilling to test it with what struck even her (in the circumstances) as a fabrication. She decided to say nothing and risk returning in time. Shortly before she left, around noon, she had second thoughts—what if she was delayed?—but he was probably in or on the way to the mess hall, and there was no way to reach him. She could not write in English. She taught Obaachan an English phrase: "Reiko go Kyoto to temple," having the old lady repeat it several dozen times. Then she gave her a hundred yen, locked up the house, and caught the rickety electric train.

Near Sanjo Station, in Kyoto, she had two straight whiskies to nerve herself. She boarded a bus for Demachiyanagi. She was, or so she felt, too chicly dressed to be anything but what she was. They stared at her and judged her, these alien hard-eyed Japanese. Slightly drunk, she could return or ignore the glances. At Demachiyanagi she took still another electric train, bound for the suburbs. The monstrous machine with the wasplike undercarriage rattled her home. Her mother and young sister met her at the station, a five-minute walk from the temple. Afterwards they went to a small noodle shop, and her mother invited her home. It was difficult to refuse. At six-thirty she slipped out and phoned the barracks, but remembered before the call went through that he would not be there. He went to church Friday nights, his part of the bargain with his room sergeant. When she returned to the house the sleeping mats were spread. Her mother made a tearful appeal. It was hours before she got away. She caught the last train from Sanjo, arrived at Hama-Hara at twelve-fifteen and phoned the comcenter from a tobacconist. Popkin wasn't there. He was working mids, and she began to worry; worried even more when she did not find him at the house, drunk, asleep, as she expected to; remained uneasy through the following week without a clear idea of what had taken place, until events engulfed the wino and there was nothing left to be concerned about.

Taub returned from the Inland Sea on Monday, in time for the evening meal. He learned almost at once that Popkin was in trouble, although no one seemed to know exactly what the poor bastard had done. It seemed right for him to be in trouble, it gave Taub a sense of clairvoyance (although it was Helver, not he, who had predicted this). Helver came into the mess hall and Taub moved to join him. The lawyer would have the inside scoop. Taub found him by and large uncommunicative.

"But what's the upshot?"

"Everything's under control. He didn't take it, he wasn't driving. He'll get off lightly, I think, off post without a pass. Unless," he said, more to himself, "Akemi screws us up."

"Akemi! What's she got to do with it?"

"She was in the car. That's all I can tell you."

"What do you mean by screw us up? What can she do?"

Helver shrugged. "Excuse me, Lyle, I've got to take Kaz to the movies."

He was annoyed first with Helver, then with Akemi, who seemed responsible for Helver's reticence. His dislike for Popkin faded in front of the larger thing, the girl's seeming ability to cause disaster. Her Friday outrage burned anew in him; he had done less than justice, at the time, to its enormity.

Well, he was still on pass; he'd go see Akemi. Maybe he could play a role in saving the old man's luckless part-Jewish hide.

Around the corner from Jackie's Bar Friday night Popkin fell into a concrete ditch running parallel to the road. The right trouser leg of his khakis was wet through to the thigh, he scraped some skin from the side of his calf, but was not otherwise damaged. As he picked himself up an MP patrol jeep turned the corner, pulled up and stopped beside him.

"Need any help?"

"No," Popkin said. He knew better than accept favors from snotnosed MPs. He walked with dignity back toward the camp, his eyes fixed on the chimney top straight ahead. Now a house loomed. That he walked at a sixty-degree angle to the road he discovered by tripping over the ditch on the other side and sprawling into the underbrush. He let the MP grip his shoulder.

"No sweat Jack, a free ride back home."

"All right then," Popkin said. "If it gives you pleasure."

The MP, as he said, simply meant to take the rummy home. His buddy, a lean, young blond, seemed to disapprove of the operation but said nothing. Popkin was sure he smelled liquor on his breath.

"Where you been drinkin'?"

"What?"

"Man you reek. Drinkin' on duty. Serious offense. You better kill it with this." The bottle had somehow survived; he pulled it from his back pocket and thrust it, from the back of the jeep, across the blond MP's chest. The MP pushed it away.

"Don't wise off, Pop," the boy said. He added, "We went off duty five minutes ago." Then he said, "Dad, let's see your pass."

So the first interior Popkin visited was not HQ Company's barracks (if he had planned returning there) but the desk sergeant's office. The desk sergeant scowled at Popkin until they were alone.

"Goddamn it, a man your age leaving post without his pass."

"Now wait up, Frank. How in hell old you think I am?"

"Look, Lester, you're crocked."

"No argument."

"You just been in trouble recently. If I write you up, it might go hard with you. I make you an offer. Go straight back and hit the sack, in the barracks I mean. Stay put there until the morning. And this little incident dies right here. But if I let you off, and you're seen again offpost to-night . . ."

"I'm a reasonable man," Popkin said. "Anyway, I go on duty at midnight. Till then, I could damn well use couple hours sleep."

"All right, get the hell out now. Just remember what I said."

Popkin went outside. The MPs who brought him in had gone. He wobbled smartly toward the barracks, counting cadence, across the parade field. He entered the barracks and left at once through the rear door. He stared at the cross above the chapel, at the service club, at the not yet visible jeep-sized hole in the fence beyond.

When she was not home now, the third time, he decided to go to bed. It was ten-fifteen, and an hour's sleep or so before going on mids was, as he told the desk sergeant, reasonable. The CQ was not in the orderly room. Awaiting his return, to ask to be wakened at twenty to twelve, Popkin succumbed to the telephone. In the midst of his call the CQ returned.

"Is Lieutenant Frick over there?"

"I'm sorry, he hasn't come in yet. I believe he's working late tonight. Who's calling, please?"

"This here is Major Dawes."

"This is his wife, Major. Did you ring earlier in the evening?"

"No. I'm a busy man."

"Is there a message?"

"No message," Popkin said. He smiled at the CQ, who waited to pounce: "Major Dawes," he said, "you're Popkin?"

"That's it."

"I got a call from the desk sergeant a couple of minutes ago that you're supposed to be in bed. I have just come down from your room."

"I was making my toilet," Popkin said. "But I'm retiring now."

"You'd best be. I'll be up for a look in five minutes' time."

"*Daijobe*," Popkin said. "You're only doin' your job."

Despite the rush, climbing the stairs, of fatigue-banishing resentment, Popkin loved the Army: he proved this, after changing his trousers in the darkened room, by propping pillow and spare blanket and underclothes under the covers in a shape vaguely like a man's. He thumped down the stairway and into the night. Behind the barracks a rocky footpath lost itself in the hills. He followed it. He planned, after a while, to sit in the cool, silent darkness, inside the camp yet out of it. But the trail curved sharply after thirty yards and led him out into the clearing occupied by the officers' club.

Popkin sighed. A man could not escape the brass, even during off-duty hours. The silence which had misled him was suddenly shattered by a tinny rendering of "Sentimental Reasons," a halfnote away from the true melody. He watched couples rise and move out to the dance floor. According to Helver, Frick was in there too, no more with Reiko than Popkin was himself; but he knew better now. Great invention, the telephone. But he had not wanted to think about this again until he had to, which was why he wandered up into the mountain.

The smooth, green lawn lured him. He sat in its center, drained the whiskey bottle and tossed it in a high arc off toward the side of the building. A second later it crashed on chrome and steel. Popkin lay back on the grass. He moaned, "Why did I down all that rotgut at one time."

Lying down only made the world spin round. He staggered off to where the bottle had smashed and relieved himself. He bent to inspect the damage done by the bottle and found only a small scratch on the right rear fin. It was a cream-colored convertible, a beautiful car. He had not seen it at Hara before. Doubtless it belonged to a light-bird or above, and as he had nothing against light-birds and above, he was glad he had not damaged it much. He walked clear around it twice. The third time the button clicked smartly under his thumb, the door swung gently open, and Popkin lowered himself into the driver's seat.

Probably, if the key had not been in the ignition, he would not have thought to take it for a spin. The last time he had driven a car was four years ago, and he never felt easy behind a wheel. But this was a magic machine: to turn the key started it up, the power steering moved to a touch. "Lights," he said, fiddling with the dash until the lights came on. He spun the big car around to face the roadway. He kept it moving at a careful ten to fifteen miles an hour. It nosed into camp between the barracks and the snack bar. He ducked low as two signal men came out of the snack bar. At the main gate he straightened and returned a salute from an imaginary MP as he glided past the empty booth. "I'll be in the area all day," Popkin said. "Make way for General Dawes."

The *densha* rattled by just as the Cadillac turned onto the road. It was surprisingly quick, the ancient, two-car electric train, and he abandoned the contest after a hundred yards because of how hard it was to keep the car on the left side of the road. Got to obey that assbackwards law, he thought for your own safety as well. A traffic light checked him on the camp side of the canal. Waiting, he put on his glasses and inspected the dashboard. He found the knob he wanted, pushed, and the top slid smoothly down. On green he jolted across the bridge, along the route he had followed earlier in the evening. This brought him onto the shopping street, a strictly pedestrian thoroughfare. There was barely any clearance as he eased the huge car down the bumpy road. He pulled up outside the flickering neon sign which spelled out Jackie's Bar.

Once, pre-Reiko, he had been fairly friendly with Akemi, but would not have gone to see her now had the meeting with Taub and Helver, in front of the bar, not planted the name in his mind. He craved uncritical company, to make a nice appearance in the front seat of the general's car. He had no money left, but once more there was nothing he wanted to buy.

Akemi was one of two girls in the bar. The other slept over a magazine; Akemi was occupied. She sat next to a burly blond in civvies who appeared unconscious. His cheek rested on the tabletop. To his profile she applied the business end of a cigarette. Occasionally he groaned and slapped his face. When she had to she removed his hand and patiently, gingerly resumed.

Popkin slid into the seat opposite and watched for a time.

"What the hell you doing, Akemi."

She glanced up.

"Hello, Pop. Why you don't mind your own business, *ne?*"

"Sorry."

She relented: "I give MP Mickey Finn. Now I write Japanese word for butterfly because I think he step out on me this week. He is a no good son of a bitch."

Suddenly the troop bolted upright, as if shamming all the time. But his eyes betrayed him. Popkin recognized the face of the snotnose who asked him for his pass (a lightning change into civilian clothes), life's stinking little ironies.

"I'm a no good son of a bitch," the MP said.

"That's all right," Popkin said. "So long as you know about it."

"A son of a bitch," he repeated, his face banging forward on the tabletop. Akemi reached into his shirt pocket for the cigarettes. She lit one, puffed it to a rosy glow, resumed.

While the scene was not without interest, Popkin felt moved to intervene. This he did carefully.

"I think you should knock off, Akemi, and come riding in my new car."

She paused. "You have convertible?"

"Bet your ass. Go take a look outside."

"A good idea," she said. "Jackie already go home, so no sweat. Okay, if he can come too."

"Him?"

"Him, yes, my boy friend, butterfly MP. We drive very fast, open door, drop him into fucking lake."

"Well now." He appeared to think this over. "We don't want no trouble now."

"If he come I come," Akemi said. "Or the whole world stay here."

"Ah hell, he can come."

They got the MP to his feet, moaning and blowing out his crimson cheek, and maneuvered him into the front seat of the car. "Where you steal this car, old man?" she asked cannily. "You're wrong about that, Akemi, the general lend it to me." She sat between them, the MP slumped heavily on her shoulder. "Drive that way." She pointed toward the camp. "That way is Tokyo." "Jesus," Popkin said, "a gallon of black coffee now would suit me fine."

The contents of the glove compartment had spilled into the front seat, where the MP had been. So Helver learned almost immediately whose car it was. Akemi sprawled on her belly across the hood, her hands locked protectively behind her head. The MP lay face upward in the dirty shallows. Popkin sat, as he had been, in the driver's seat, his hands gripping the wheel.

"Why'd you take his car?" Helver said. "What did that accomplish?"

"You think I did it on purpose?" Popkin said. "I been havin' this trouble all night, which way is straight ahead. But I was doin' fairly well until now."

"You're not driving," Helver said. "You're not even here. You've been with me. Now come, come." With strong, chubby arms he hoisted Popkin toward him, out of the driver's seat.

"Where you think you going, *Debuchan?*" She rolled onto her side, supporting herself on an elbow. "That old man son of a bitch spoil my new skirt. Look, I think MP is dead."

"He's breathing," Helver said. "How would you like ten thousand yen for a new dress?"

"You pull my leg, *ne?*"

"Listen closely," Helver said. "The MP was driving. Do you understand me? They will ask you who drove the car and you will say it was the MP. For ten thousand yen in cash. Will you do it?"

"If I say MP drive car you give me ten thousand yen? When you pay?"

"Tomorrow morning," Helver said. "Believe me, Akemi. Listen to me. You and Popkin were sitting in Jackie's. The MP came and picked you up in the car. Do you have that?" he hissed at Popkin, who looked up with horror and unbelief from the white laminated card. "My god, it's Frick's. But I didn't take it. I wasn't driving." He stared slack-mouthed with shock and gratitude. *Good,* Helver thought. *So he does not screw himself.* He went to drag the slim blond boy out of the water just as a Japanese policeman and two MPs began to descend the embankment.

5

Unreasonable to hold the four who turned up responsible for the others' defection, but he couldn't help it: hate welled in him for Frankel, Teller, Michaelson, and Bernstein, caused him to falter in a treble, sputter off into silence on the word *Adonai.* Because twenty men had shipped home the day before, including a regular and two possibles (with one of

whom he'd had frequent success); since he felt fairly certain of his half-dozen, and expected, at this point needed no
more; Taub had omitted the pre-service ritual, the whim-
sical search for the Jews. So reaped his reward now, this
anaemic quartet behind him. Failing to meet even his own
adjusted minimum, the fruits of compromise, six skull-capped
men without *talaisim* in worse than an empty room, a barely
converted heathen temple. Yet he had gone ahead, with
loathing, less for the absentees than for Frankel, Teller,
Michaelson, and Bernstein, who looked up with interest and
a trace of critical surprise when he faltered and stopped in
the midst, at the height of a prayer.

He did not resume. In his shoulders and the back of his
head they might read, if they were able, the persecuting
weight of centuries, rabbinical prodigies of patience and
mute despair. But when he turned, with a weary smile, he
had molded a thing to be, from the stuff of dignity, disgust,
and fellowship.

"Gentlemen. Your forbearance. I consider it pointless to
continue. Where I erred, doubtless, was in beginning with
less than a quorum; I was under the misapprehension that
one or two more would drift in before we moved too far
along. Under the circumstances . . . I suggest we follow
the custom, each man praying silently at his own speed until
he concludes."

It took them by surprise. "Tie it up, Lyle," Bernstein said
(New York humor, guying common sense). "We have
enough *frumkeit* here for ten."

Taub smiled. "I would rather we stopped. We could
continue, but my heart would not be in it. If one of the congregation is willing or able to take over, naturally I raise no
objection," since things can become no more farcical than

they are. "No volunteers? *Lachah dodee lekras kalah*," he sang, turned and unhinged his knees, signaling the abrupt plunge into the ultimate acreage of private, silent prayer.

Popkin's heart wasn't in it either fifteen minutes earlier when he took the shortcut behind the service club, his hands deep in his pockets, whistling tonelessly, so much out of it in fact that he questioned his own sanity. *This is no good either*, he thought; *I'm going to ruin myself*, walking too casually through the dusk past countless windows, visible to anyone inside who might want to reflect, "Popkin? Restricted indefinitely to the post? Courting trouble still another time?" and yet be unaware, this observer, that for three hours past, since Helver yanked him away from the day-room pool table, gave him the news as the pink, fat color faded from his face, the issue was merely would he seek trouble, or would he wait around and let it find him. But no one saw Lester Popkin from the service-club or library windows.

At first he had waited, as Helver had not even had to advise; shot pool by himself from two to five-thirty waiting for his name through the loudspeaker, refusing to think of what Helver had told him or what he, in a matter of moments, could say to Frick; blanked his mind to the new, deeper trouble. By five-forty-five, when he had still not been called, he put down his cue and went to the snack bar. Here, unable to eat, he succumbed to the hopelessness, gave in to the old impotent rage at their trickery. The old rage came on him, for Frick, sleek and plotting, like the goddamn Gestapo, waiting to haul him in at midnight maybe, or the day after, or the day after that, when his guard was down, at their leisure, because Pop? Restricted to the post forever, he ain't going nowhere.

This was what incensed him: that despite knowing all, they used the fact of his restriction to dawdle over punishment. The restriction itself, imposed one week before, he never objected to—a chronic offender caught off post without his pass, he had been liable, even for that small offense, to much graver penalties. (The MP, elected by a three-fourths majority as driver of the stolen car, remembering nothing and having said as much, awaited court-martial and the completion of Frick's investigations in Camp Hara's makeshift jail.) Restriction had not even inconvenienced him much. The good things came to him. Every night at eight Reiko (known now to be innocent; bringing wine) came on post and met him outside the enlisted men's club. After a couple of drinks there they walked back across the road and climbed into the hills, behind the barracks. Here, on a GI blanket, to background music from the officers' club, on a gentle slope, he drank wine and they made love. She was due this evening as well. But tonight, Popkin thought, we'll dance in bed; I've had it either way, I ain't going to hang around. He bolted his coffee, walked swiftly to the barracks, changed into a Hawaiian sport shirt and light blue trousers. I'm out of my mind, he thought, nearing the wire fence (after all, there are degrees of misfortune)—but he did not turn back; instead he adopted a comical (should anyone have seen), a much too casual air.

At which moment Taub's under-populated Friday service began. Now it nears its abortive end: *"Git Shabbus,"* says Bernstein, first and too loudly, announcing his disenchantment and his reading speed. Taub smiles privately, without real pleasure. He prays on. Though he has abdicated the headship he remains at a height up front, his rear parts toward the group. These he manipulates with fresh violence, cheeks jutting toward the first row, where Frankel and Teller sit—this signifies that he too nears the end. "*Gut Shabbus, gut Shabbus,*" at last he turns. Bernstein has made for the door, the others mill about with no real hope. Taub thinks: the *shnurrers*, but contains himself. There will be other Fridays, larger turnouts than this one in his remaining twelve weeks at Hara, if he does not alienate this trio here. "I think we'll skip the *kiddush*, gentlemen, since this is something less than an official gathering and," he smiles, "I honestly forgot the wine. By next week things ought to be back to normal. Which reminds me. Has anyone seen Helver, or Popkin? I'm amazed that neither turned up tonight."

But no one has. Taub lags behind, collects the prayer books, switches off the lights. He steps out and locks the door. Twelve weeks—he has not really considered how close he is to going home. To his parents, to a last year of rabbinical training, to familiar things. His spirits lift. He walks slowly along the base of the mountain, and from somewhere drums up an inkling of regret. They have not been bad, his sixteen months in this part of the world—no reasonably sensitive person who has lived there can help feeling deeply for Japan. Already he feels nostalgia, what will be nostalgia, as he sits at the kitchen table on Jerome Avenue and tries to re-create, for parochial family and friends, sixteen months in the Far East. He will not dwell long on the clichés, cherry blossoms, geisha, sacred mountain, but instead . . . on the other things. They'll be there when he needs them, in perspective and retrospect, the many things he has observed and learned which, immersed as he is in them still, are now not so easy to isolate. In spite of his initial chagrin at being expelled from Georgia, he must now feel something like gratitude toward the Army for sending him overseas.

Gratitude. That slob Popkin showed gratitude by missing the service tonight—but this Taub must dismiss. For
Popkin cannot yet know he has real cause to be grateful.
He is unaware that Taub has suffered in pride, pocket, and
time; so he cannot have stayed away through thanklessness.
Perhaps he'll never know, Taub thinks, or I at least will never
tell him—a kindness in a case like this is its own best reward.

It begins to rain as he comes even with the barracks. His
thoughts have turned him restless; he'll pick up his pass, his
bamboo and oil-paper umbrella, catch the bus to Kyoto,
and walk the streets awhile. He's fond of the city, redolent
of ancient glory, although turning a face to the uninitiate of
modernity and noise, cars and cabarets. He'll go in and feel
the centuries pulse around him. There are so many temples,
gardens, shrines he still has not seen. He'd use his time more
wisely, given a second chance. All the same, he wishes he
were going home soon, tomorrow, now. The foretaste of
nostalgia grips him more.

The imponderables complicate thought, so he hums a
little. He's almost wholly in the dark, recall, and she might
not even be there. Or there and bleary-eyed, there hating
his soul. Pathetic, ruined, and bad: once he ignored these
things because of wit, but were they the price she paid for
being so *amusante?* The necessary foil for her to seem to be?
Likely, very likely. Although—he's no hypocrite—abomina-
ting her now, he need not scourge himself for admiring her
once. She was truly entertaining, in his partial knowledge.
But now, her badness threatens change. Helver told him.
He plans to ascertain, by whatever means (the imponderables
complicate thought), that she bring no harm, through malice
or carelessness, to one of his own. And he hates her all

right. He will not neglect the chance, should it arise (he hums a little), to crush her too.

It's soon after the supper hour, and a Monday, but a half-dozen GIs are in the cabaret. This is Standard Operating Procedure near payday. Some have been there most of the day, others, less lucky, have come straight from work, bypassing the mess hall for the fried rice and friendship that money can buy. Jackie's staff is ten strong for all of this week which means that four girls, as Taub enters, are not occupied. One rises, comes up and reaches for his hand. Doubtless a new *kourve,* or she'd know the score and leave him alone. This is how things are in bars: once you make your choice you've made it, for better or worse, and even if your girl is busy while others are not you'll be left alone until she's able or chooses to join you. "You come sit down?" says the tart. Taub is not unkind. "I'm a friend," he says, "of Akemi. Excuse me. Sorry." He disengages himself and walks to the bar. Jackie is there, guarding the bottles and the unoccupied stools. Taub sits. "*Konban wa,*" he says.

"Good evening," Jackie replies, "how you? Akemichan!" she yells over the music's roar. "A beer, please," says Taub. "*Nani?*" Akemi calls. Jackie inclines her head toward Taub. Taub can make out no reply.

"Let's dance, Akemi," says someone, and there is shuffling behind him on the dance floor. Naturally he doesn't expect her to join him at once; Jackie has merely alerted her, if she cares, that the last arrival is one of her own. Still, she should acknowledge him, Taub feels, angry or not. But he does not turn round. Jackie pours his beer. She reminds him of a football player he sat next to in a History of Religion course. He looks away, toward the back of the room. Now he can see her dancing from the corner of his eye. Recalling his mission, he feels superior to the game. He turns and stares.

Over her partner's shoulder she smirks at him; more this, he decides, than a scowl or a frown. "*Kaerusan,*" she says, "*kechinbō,*" and whispers something in the GI's ear. He spins her around and his tough, dull eyes take in Taub. He laughs. "Naw," he says. "He don't look like one to me."

Taub turns back around. Control, he thinks, a duty to perform. Sticks and stones, he thinks, but his pulse smacks in his temples. There's a shriek from the floor, followed by a giggle, then the voice of the leprechaun: "Son of a bitch. You goose me in public. Cost you five hundred yen."

"Naw, Akemi. You ain't got enough tail make it worth while."

"Then you buy me drink."

"Just bought you one. You drink 'em too fast. All water anyway."

One second later she stood by Taub, her bony elbows on the bar. "*Konban wa, Kaerusan. Comment allez-vous?*"

"Hello, Akemi."

She squeezed his upper arm.

"You feel like beat me up again tonight?"

"I never touched you, Akemi. I hope that's clear in your mind."

"*Dorinku katte kurehen?*"

Taub nods.

"Vodka collins, *chōdai,*" she says to Jackie, who mixes and serves.

"Come sit in booth," Akemi says. "Same price. We shoot the shit awhile."

Three large, boisterous troops enter the bar.

"I want to talk to you, Akemi, but preferably outside."

"Outside? What for? Nothing to drink outside."

"Then finish up your drink and we'll go somewhere else. It's too crowded here."

"*Detara akan*," Jackie says. "Very busy now. She must work here."

"Just for ten minutes," Taub says.

"*Dekimahen*. She work here till eleven. Then she can go where she want."

In his hand he clutches eight hundred yen, his change from a thousand-yen note. He pockets the three hundreds, carefully folds the five-hundred-yen note in four. He places this unsmiling near Jackie's hand.

"*Sore wa nan desu no?*" She is arch.

"*Presento*. If she can come outside for twenty minutes."

"*Sore dake?*" the fullback flashes him a golden smile. "*Happyaku en nara, nan toka*," she says.

All right. The hungry whore. $2.22 more. He takes out the three hundred yen, places it with the five on the bar. With amazement, Akemi has watched this odd exchange.

"What's up, *Kaeru?* For my part, I don't want to go anywhere."

Ah God, no trouble with her, Taub pleads.

"Suppose we sit up front then in the restaurant. Believe me, Akemi, it's highly important."

"*Shōchi shimasu*," she says. "*Itte kimasu*," she calls to the group. She picks up her drink and leads the way.

A family of four sits toward the front of the restaurant. They eat ice cream. The two small children regard the materialized Taub with amazement, tug at mother's kimono sleeve. Taub lowers himself deliberately at a rear table, nearest to the bar. Akemi sits opposite. He waves the waiter away, stares the adults (but not the children) down. Music is audible, from the world inside, but not disturbing. He looks a long while at Akemi (he has her now) with humor, compassion, understanding, hatred, love.

She breaks it up: "You feel hot to go?"

"No," Taub says. He even smiles. "I'd like to know, first of all, what you whispered, concerning me I think, to the friend you were just dancing with. You know I'm interested in your strange little mind."

"*Are!*" she says. "Of course." She thinks. "I said to him . . . *chotto matte, ne* . . . I said, 'You see fat ugly troop sit at bar?' "

Taub waits.

" 'He number one muffdiver in Japan.' Now you know I can go back to bar, *ne?*"

"Wait!" Taub says. He reaches out and encircles her wrist. "We're not finished. That was incidental. Something totally different is on my mind."

"*Ah sō ka.* Must be *takusan* important, too, you pay eight hundred yen."

"You can be sure it is. Please pay careful attention to what I say. It's about Popkin and your accident Friday night. And the matter of the stolen car." He gropes for knowledge as he sets the scene. Helver is once more inwardly cursed for leaving him so deeply in the dark. Akemi and Popkin and an unidentified thief-driver crash in Frick's car sometime Friday night after Taub and Helver leave Jackie's Bar; and Akemi is not trusted to give an accurate account of the scene. This last part he can fasten on, how well he conceives it to be true.

"What accident?"

"Akemi, act your age. I know all about the accident so I ask you, don't play games."

"Nobody got hurt," she said. "Very small accident."

"The Army takes a different view," said Taub. "Stealing an officer's car is a serious offense, let alone smashing it up. The guilty party will be heavily punished."

"You break my heart."

"All right. He doubtless deserves it. That's precisely why we have to guard against mistakes. So that the right man receives his punishment."

She looks surprised. "You know MP?"

"What MP?"

"Corporal Baker, you jerk, we all go for ride in convertible car."

Click! in that sensitized brain, the secret he has pretended to know: her hot pants, her blind passion for MPs, this is what the lawyer fears. That's why she can't be trusted. Doubly so, for this Baker was certainly a friend.

"No, I don't think I know him," says Taub.

"Then what you worry about, *Kaeru*," she says. He shakes her in the mind's eye, slaps her hard, and says, I worry for Popkin, slut, my *lansman*, my friend.

"No one is worried, Akemi. There's no reason to be, yet. You've already talked to the authorities, have you?"

"*Hai.* Lieutenant see me Friday night. I tell him what I know."

"I see. You told the truth about who stole the car."

For a split second fear pays a visit to that small, pretty face. She sips her drink, wipes her mouth, and shrugs her shoulders. "*Mochiron yo.* Akemi never lie."

But he's caught it, and it thrills him, for while it ought to mean she has already done or contemplates doing a disservice to the truth, he had despaired of making her afraid. Things have been very shaky from the start; but at least, at last, the bitch knows fear. He would love to work that vein, dilate that fear, then free her from it before she can do so (in her awful resilience) on her own.

But she has already done so. All the same, he slaps his

billfold on the table. Thousand-yen notes, too big for the wallet, protrude. He rotates it on the table. Akemi gulps her drink and half rises. "Corporal *Kaeru*," she says, "you make me bored. What do you want?"

His plan, to call it that, is new. It came to him moments before, when he bought her out of the bar. It's far from foolproof. It is, frankly, as much a gesture as a plan. But he feels it to be right: he knows already the warmth and the pain, the enriching agony of sacrifice.

"I wish to make a purchase. This will not be a new experience, you are in the habit of selling service, *deshō?* For fifteen hundred yen, is it not, we could go off and share a delightful, sordid time."

"Out of the question. Tonight you must pay twenty-five hundred."

"That's fine. You know that that is not what I ask of you. Although what I do ask I'm willing to pay well for. I want to be *absolutely certain* you've told the truth about the accident. No, don't speak, listen. I'm ready to give you five thousand, repeat, five thousand yen for this certainty. Now: if you've already told the truth, consider this money a reward, yours to keep with no questions asked; if you've in any way lied—I don't ask you now if you have—you're being paid to undo the damage. Go and see Lieutenant Frick and tell him what really happened. Ring him up, I'll give you his office number. Tell the truth, whatever your personal feelings in the matter. You're not a stupid girl. You know it's wrong to harm an innocent man. Is it a bargain, Akemi?"

He stares into her face, but fails to see that he has hit her where she lives: for the second time in four nights (and the first only dimly remembered—something occurred that angered him and lit up life for her with brief startling clarity) he has indicated order, meaning, guideposts, in this crazy souped-up world. Since the incident, which she looked upon (in its unfolding) as a way to punish the MP for infidelity, she has suffered less from remorse than from a sense of self-betrayal; for at heart she is not really a vindictive soul. She was fuddled by a transient grudge and the rapidity of events—the accident, Helver's offer, the immediate interview with Frick—and now, because of what she said, the child Baker would go to jail for a thousand years. But she'd taken the step. The money, duly delivered Saturday morning, did not matter so much as the bargain itself, and that not so much as laziness. Inertia and honor held her back, not greed, or fear.

And now came this plump instigation to repair the damage, bearing funds. Arrives this divine prig with an obscure cause which sets straight her own. *Voilà!* Child of impulse, she will do it: contact, confer with, unbeguile the Law. She shakes with what for her is rare, silent laughter.

He studies his wallet now. He counts out the fresh bills, one to five. Pushes them toward her, lifts her hand and puts it on the pile.

"It's a deal then, Akemi."

From the money she looks doubtfully up at Taub. "Not too goddamn much here, *Kaerusan*. I can remember, these days, when I get more for doing less. But," she says, "you an old friend and . . ." she remembers! "you a Jew. *Dakara sa*, I give cut-rate price to tell the truth."

"Good," Taub said. Immured, immune. "Exactly that. I ask no more. *Au revoir, ma petite*. Take no drugs excessively harmful to the health."

"Stay loose." *Bakayarō*, Akemi said.

6

Popkin listened to the voices. The outer door was open, revealing the unfloored corridor that ran the length of the house, the crockery and the kerosene stove, the basins of water she drew from the well outside. The two rooms in which they lived were off to the left and higher, cut off from the "kitchen" by sliding doors. These were drawn shut; beneath them, neatly, two pairs of thonged sandals, beyond them the mournful voices. He took off his own shoes. Probably, this was for the best. She knew damn well he was restricted to the post. With a guest, she'd be less likely to press for details. He pulled back the doors. Reiko sat on the mats, propped against the wall. The other girl sat in the only chair. He had seen her before, but he couldn't place her. He avoided Reiko's glance, stepped over her legs and went into the bedroom. From beneath the double bed he pulled out a cardboard carton, from this took a bottle of wine. He carried it to the sitting room and dropped down next to Reiko. "Well," he said. "Home sweet home."

The other one had been crying, but he thought he would overlook this, at least until they were reintroduced. Two tears worked loose just then and ran a jagged course down the sides of her flat, oily nose. He turned to Reiko. "What's wrong with your friend?"

He was shaken to see she was not far from tears herself. "What's going on?"

"What you do? Scape from monkey house?"

"What monkey house? You know I wasn't in no jail."

"You suppose be in jail now."

"Who in hell told you that? Who is this?"

Kazuko snuffled. "I friend your *tomodachi* Helversan."

"Bob's girl, that's it. We met once over at the service club. What you cryin' for?"

"Why she cry *ka!*" Reiko exploded. "She cry because for two years she have one boy friend, no have nothing from today. She cry because half GIs stupid, other half sonabitch. She cry because she have good boy friend, sergeant, kind. Now Lieutenant Frick take away stripes, send him Korea, maybe Taiwan. You know why? Because *you* steal car. Because you no-good, drunk, selfish, shit. Everything your fault. So I no can cry."

She turned away. Kazuko reached out a hand, pulled it back, ran her sleeve across her eyes. "*Chigau wa, chigau wa.* Not his fault. My boy friend make big mistake. He lawyer, suppose be smart, *ne*, he want to help you, why he trust whore? Whore always make trouble. Akemi go see lieutenant other day tell him everything. She no give back money too. Now you in big trouble, Bobby too. He only want to help you. Now he must go *sayonara* . . . good-by . . ." Sobs choked her off. Popkin took a long drink of wine. Reiko kept her face turned away.

Popkin felt terrible. What was the sense of going AWOL to walk into this? She thought because she had a steady shack and Akemi assed around there was a difference between them. Everybody had a name for everybody else. He took another drink of wine.

"Ah, Akemi's all right. Who in hell knows why she switched her story. It's the stinking Army. . . ."

"Why you no tell me you steal car?" Reiko said. "To take a ride with whore."

Popkin hightailed it to the bedroom and came back with a bottle of wine. The first was half full, but he was looking ahead. "Anyone care for a drink?"

"Why you no tell me, ah?"

"You know goddamn well why. That was the day you went to your old man's grave. I didn't know where in hell you were. I needed somebody to talk to."

To his disgust, Kazuko sobbed harder and buried her face in her hands.

"Trouble with you broads, you grow attached. You call yourselves 'business girls,' but you're too soft. That's why a kid like Akemi does the smart thing. She works in a bar, she stays independent. When a beau gets sent to the big eight she figures this is life, and picks up on somebody else. Now you two will do the same friggin' thing when me and Helver go. But you have to get over it first. You have to bawl awhile. So you think that makes you different from a whore." To shut himself up he went to work on the wine.

Reiko said, "You like Akemi *ka?*"

He tore at the foil of the second bottle.

"You catch Akemi *ka?* I go way one day, Kyoto temple, you make love *panpan* work in bar."

"That ain't true," Popkin said glumly. "We just went for a lousy drive in the car."

"I no believe you. You catch her many times before, *ne*. You answer, you catch Akemi before?"

"Yeah," Popkin said. "Can't a guy have a past?"

"*Kamahen.* You can have past. Because you no have nothing else. You can take Akemi to monkey house." She stood, stormed into the bedroom, and banged shut the doors.

Kazuko looked up. "GIs all time same," she said. "All time do bad thing Japanese girl. Go back home, mess up, go with Japanese whore. GIs all time no good, all time hurt Japanese girl."

Popkin rose. They were even now, they had exchanged their views. "Why don't you go home now. Helver needs you. This might be mine and Reiko's last night together. You ought to respect that. But you come cryin' over here and spillin' the beans. Why don't you be a good kid and buzz off."

The doors squealed apart and Reiko flew into the room. "She my friend, she can stay! She go home when she want, not when you say!"

Kazuko protested in Japanese.

"*Iya*," Reiko said. "I don't care. He say Japanese girl soft, always fall in love. I no in love. Crazy old man, PFC, drink too much . . . look! He stay here twenty minutes, already finish near two bottles wine. You . . . PFC!"

"I ain't going to stand for that," Popkin said. "Abuse in my own goddamn house. I'm goin' for a walk. Maybe I'll come back, maybe not. You don't seem to give a damn either way." But she was right: he had finished nearly two bottles in record time, and didn't feel a thing. It would hit him at once within the next quarter of an hour, a devastating blow, but there was no help for it now. He stepped down into his shoes, leaving them unlaced, and turned back into the room. Reiko stood in its center, her arms straining toward him, anguish large on her simple face, and terror. Which was how it ought to be. "Send your friend home," Popkin said gently. "I'll be back in ten minutes. Just going to clear my head," and walked outside. He went to the mouth of the alley, waited, then made his way back to the house. He'd wait around until Kazuko left. He stood in the tall grass along the side, peering in at the window. They huddled a foot apart on the straw mats, balled against their grief, canceling grief by canceling themselves. They took up no room, made no sound.

He'd take his walk. This much was certain—he would lose Reiko hard. When he went back to the house he was going back to stay. He'd hole up there until they found him; not do their work for them by running back to the post and waiting with his finger up for Frick's whim to lower the boom. Another AWOL on top of the theft-perjury charge could not hurt him now, if he cared. He should return at once and tell her the news, have her lay in supplies, but better to wait until the other had definitely gone; took her tears, the world she called up he no longer had the stomach for, out into the night; so he staggered along the mesh fence which separated this part of the camp from the Japanese town. Beyond the dispensary the familiar landmark caught his eye, reaching into the drizzle and mist, and he recalled that for the first time since the bargain was struck he had let a Friday pass without depositing his body in the chapel. As he stood there the lights went out, the door swung open, and Taub stepped into the rain. Popkin watched him lock up and walk toward the barracks. "We're all square, Rabbi." Popkin said. "No more house of worship; no more bedcheck worries for me. I don't owe you a miserable thing." Then, suddenly very drunk, he came out onto the main road.

Across and to the left was the football field. It extended by one hundred fifty yards the eastern half of Camp Hara, facing for its length souvenir shops, an off-limits restaurant, two laundries, a dozen limp and tired shacks, the last outpost of the town. The railway tracks ran between the playing field and the houses, alongside the road. Here a ditch contained them; further up they climbed and leveled with the road, and a Japanese security guard stood from nine until six between the main gate and the bus depot regulating traffic as the antiquated trolley clanged a warning and lumbered by. As Popkin waited in the rain and darkness a northbound train shrieked past a crossing somewhere below the camp, came into sight a moment later, left the hollow for the level stretch and sank again as it neared him, its round eye freezing a cone of rain. Then it was past, slowing, clanking to a stop at the small station just past the football field. An Army bus coughed out of the depot and turned south, Kyoto bound. A farmer rolled by behind him with a nightsoil-laden mule, then a GI passed with his girl. Standing there was fairly risky. Soon he'd head back to the house and begin hiding out, whether or not Helver's girl was there. To be recognized now would be the death of his plans. Someone yelled, "Hey you! Buddy!" the voice of disaster, right smack on schedule, and, outraged, he slipped and slid down the grassy slope on his back and behind until he reached level ground. He was unharmed. He'd been startled, tripped on his laces, lost control, but once down he shucked shoulders and hips and helped himself to the bottom of the grade. Out of sight and reach of whoever had called. He lay there, proud of himself, tasting the rain. The wine throbbed in his head, and he closed his eyes. That was much better—not sickening as the week before. I'm holding it better, he thought; but that had been rotgut, not the sweet, familiar wine. The throbbing seemed friendly, sedative, like the sound of a familiar clock. He'd rest there a moment until it was safe to return. He drew a leg to his body, extended the other, threw his arm across his eyes. Vivid pictures raced through his brain. The throbbing softened, ceased. The rain fell harder. Popkin slept.

*May your father turn like a roasting pig over eternal
flames. Let the host devour your whore-mother's breast at
a leisurely clip. Cholera and lesser plagues infect your kin.
I pray you should lose your means of livelihood.* Old World
imprecations in ascending practical order batter the Asiatic's
head, for he isn't blind. To get the job he must pass a rig-
orous eye test, and for a moment, approaching and exiting
from opposite gates, they faced each other across the narrow road. To avoid the ghost of misunderstanding he began
to trot as well as wave the umbrella, stepped ankle-deep in
a puddle, and was wet through in both directions by the
rain. What *chutzpah!* He all but shakes his fist at the bus's
brown behind as it veers left, yards away, and rumbles
toward the town. Almost no one is aboard. Granted there
are rules; granted he wasn't at the stop in time; no harm
would befall the man for relenting in such weather. Com-
plaining to the Transportation Officer does not really enter
his mind, but the driver of even a military vehicle should be
able to distinguish when legality is not the higher form of
wisdom.

So there he stands. Chagrined? Enraged? As the bus dis-
appears he adjusts to the busless world with the efficient
languor of an animal, Out of sight, out of mind. The Japanese driver need not be forgiven who has never sinned. The
densha will see him through. The *densha* goes by the small,
local station every quarter of an hour. If it makes for a
longer, less comfortable ride it at the same time launches
his plan, the invocation of an atmosphere. Better the be-
draggled townsfolk for a beginning, country bundles in the
aisles, than neat and chattering Army wives. Moments
earlier a train grumbled northward and he hears it echo still,
clattering along the lakeside. The sounds do not recede,

perhaps they blend with the noises of a nearing Kyoto train. He quickens his step, so as not to miss that too.

"You! Hey buddy!"

The building closest to him is the dispensary, set back a way from the fence. On its porch, out of the weather, stands the man who called. There seems little doubt that he is hailing Taub. The cantor slows.

"You got a match?"

"Yes."

"How about a light?"

"How do you propose I get it to you?"

"Hang on, I'll come over."

He limps through the rain, reaches through the mesh and takes the book from Taub. "Like feeding monkeys," he says. "I just this minute ran out." He cups the match, lights up, exhales. "Hell of a note. Pulled a muscle in that night problem the other week. They said I was too old to go running around in the dark, but I felt I had to do it. Fell into a hole."

"I'll need those back."

"Yeah, here. I asked some guy for a light not two minutes ago and he disappeared. He was standing right there, by the gulley. My eyesight must be goin' bad too."

"Thank you."

"Where'd you get that umbrella? I ought to pick up one like it for my wife. Just to give her a hard time. She's a Jap, yet she don't like anything gook. Not even clothes. For a minute there, I thought you was a gook yourself."

"No," Taub says. "The gooks are different from us. I must move on."

To conceal his repugnance. He leaves behind the instant intimacy of the friendless, the empty yearning of the dumb and old. Who are, to return to a favorite topic, the heart's

blood of the Army. For only fools remained (below com-
missioned level) to age gracelessly, or at all, in the self-
immolating looking-glass sub-society which has never lost a
war. But (in the present instance) redeemed as well as
damned by ignorance, married to a Japanese girl. Wonderful shoeless evenings at home, a back rub, make the rest worth
while. Life with a war child who denies her dislocated heritage from the safety of the PX while it is all around her, to
languish and die in Tulsa or Frankfurt for a piece of *sushi*
or the smell of incense or the sight of a Japanese sign.
Making dead communion with Italian war brides in Ashe-
ville and White Sands because the great white mother saw
it that way, American Army wife, imposing her tiny vision
by the simple process of majority rules. America, the melt-
ing pot. It's suicide and stupid to deny what you are. Particularly if it's etched on your face, but likewise if not—
either way they'll bury you in the end. So your suffering is
more to the point if you understand why. Acknowledge,
admit, *secretly approve*. He knows these anti-Japanese Japanese, as he knows non-Jewish Jews, and they must all reap
bupkas for their pains. Rejectors of the unrejectable, he has
met them in New York, and since. They affect indifference,
distaste, or, back to the wall, they bolster with bland egalitarian argument. And they are all, as they should be, sniffed
out in the end. For they are the Chosen People. The designa-
tion Jew will always be pejorative. There must be an out-
group. This is the divine order of things. If lucky enough
to be born one, rejoice! Savor the proud martyrdom, hate
when required, hold your head high. This is the Old Testa-
ment Message, what it means to be a Jew. This is also what
it means to be other things, but it is not necessary (even if
possible) to work up a kinship with the Underdog. Anti-
Semitism transcends. It shatters boundaries. It welds diverse

national/ethnic groups. The wife of the old regular on the dispensary porch is in trouble, but she will never know what real suffering means.

The sound builds in volume, the approach of a south-bound tram. They crossed somewhere beyond the camp, but he reaches the station in time. A few folk alight, Taub alone boards. He sits toward the front of the first car, close to the standing man who manipulates the complicated levers and bars which control the ancient train. Rows of straw seats face across the aisle. Taub adjusts the inverted umbrella between his legs, and the droplets trickle to the floor, form a pool. He studies the party opposite. It's a school-girl, engrossed in a book, her chin supported on her fist. Rose-cheeked, seventeen, sweet mouth, braided hair. Wearing the black skirt and white blouse which is the student's uniform, and wooden clogs against the rain. She reminds him in some ways of a cousin in New York, the same air of innocence. Immediately he notes the resemblance a warmth engulfs him, suffusions of self-approbation. This is odd (if pleasant), because he has thought this kind of thing, without loving himself, before: has remarked that many Japanese faces call white ones to mind, of types, usually, but often (as now) of individuals, as if in Japan he has stumbled onto a space-time continuum where one found slightly distorted mirror-images of family and friends. That's already struck him—uniformly black-haired and black-eyed, there was enough variety in their features to evoke the heterogeneous world of whites, and more: faces unduplicated outside of Asia, or Japan.

Yet now this warmth grips him. To the current observa-tion accrues an astounding moral: *We are all the same.* This mystical platitude moves him (though it sits uneasy

with the ruminations which precede). Despite himself, all
unawares, he is, has been, a bastion of brotherhood.

But he senses the glare of the girl's neighbor, a crone.
She hates him, he sees sadly, and for the wrong reasons:
all this time he has been staring at the girl. He is a con-
queror, come to rape the countryside. She doesn't need to
read his dog tags, this ancient lady, she'll judge him anyway. For the primal antagonism she, they, can look to
their own. They have their *eta*, unmentionable outcast
class, persecuted in accord with antique, hallowed laws. The
eta lives in ghettos, though no longer obliged to do so, but
both parties want it that way. The relationship has reached
an advanced stage, become, by common consent, a mutual
act of mind. The Japanese (as Helver said) do not need the
Jews.

But, this being so, neither does he need the Japanese. If
Taub, in what he conceives as his essence, is irrelevant to
these people, the opposite is likewise true. It is in being
God's eta that the Jew truly exists: supremely affirmed by
being thus divinely denied. Bother the babel of the non-
Jewish world. He's been right from the start, right both
ways. Nothing of the tortuous dialectic need be disclaimed.

He looks toward the front of the car, at the conductor's
back, where something is taking place. The man's head sinks
mollusc-like, he yells, makes frantic passes at the levers and
dials. The second car lurches into the first and Taub is
thrown into the aisle. All is confusion and overturned par-
cels and a mad sound eclipses the conductor's screams—it
is the sound of death and loneliness, and he knows, crouch-
ing at the schoolgirl's feet, the train has hit a living thing.
Already people crane from windows; conductor and ticket-
seller lower themselves through doors built for platform

level onto the tracks below. Taub looks at the girl's stiff, frightened face; he has the wild impulse to sit beside her and soothe away the sickness he feels welling up on his own. He picks himself from the floor. A hand tugs at his trouser cuff, it is the ticket-seller, below, nearly in tears: *"Amerikajin da yo. Orite kuremahen ka?"*

"So it's an American! What can I do!" But he retrieves his umbrella and suffers the man to help him through the door. He descends, pained and dreamy, keeping his face averted from the lantern and the torment. The yell breaks again from the thing on the tracks, not human, he can no longer look away.

The beam of light traps the gaping mouth and the pain-maddened eyes. The body is unharmed (men of both races will say, later, "A lucky man"), but the right foot is crushed and gone beneath the wheels. His fingernails bite deep into his skull, blood runs past his ears. He seems to be waiting; shudders; once more he screams.

On his knees, Taub digs his fists into his cheeks and through his roaring sickness indicts the might-have-been, Why, why did you not let him come to *shul?*

IVAN GOLD, born in New York
in 1932, has degrees from Col-
umbia University and from the
School of Oriental and African
Studies of the University of Lon-
don. He has lived in Japan, as
well as in England, Sweden, and
Spain, and now makes his home
in New York.